By Any Other Name

MaryJanice Davidson

Hard Shell Word Factory

For Alexander and Sharon Davidson
and
Elinor and William Along
Happily ever after.

© 2001 MaryJanice Alongi
Ebook ISBN: 1-58200-660-1
Published September 2001

Hard Shell Word Factory
PO Box 161
Amherst Jct. WI 54407
books@hardshell.com
http://www.hardshell.com
Cover art © 2001 Mary Z. Wolf

Chapter 1

STEPHANIE DARES was nervous about meeting the Darth Vader of venture capitalists, but that wasn't why she was under her desk. She was out of sight on the floor, hooking up the computer. It was slow going; there were about sixteen cords to match two outlets, not including the modem cords, and she didn't know as much about this sort of thing as she would have liked. *An MIT grad wouldn't know as much about this sort of thing as I'd like,* she thought with grim humor. *Oh, to have invested in an IMac when I had the chance.*

Still, it beat pacing, which was her only other option. She'd turned up the radio nice and loud, but it didn't lessen her annoyance. She wished Darth Vader would get here. And she hoped he'd have a surge protector with him. That would be just right. That would be just—

"Anybody here?"

She sat up at the sound and bumped her head on the underside of the desk. "Ouch!"

"Who said that?"

She crawled from under the desk and tried to stand but misjudged the length of the desktop and banged her head again. "Ouch!" she said again, louder, standing up and rubbing her head. There was a man standing in the doorway, frowning at her. She glared, instantly blaming him for her throbbing head, however irrational she knew that was. "What is it?"

"You're not from the real estate agency," he said skeptically.

"I am. Are you Darth—I mean, are you Erik Chambers?"

He scowled at her slip and she could feel the blood rushing to her face. *Newsweek* had called Chambers and Associates, and Erik Chambers in particular, the Darth Vader of venture capitalists. The article had been grudgingly complimentary but had pulled few punches. And while Stephanie had read every word and had seen the accompanying photo of Erik, she had been unprepared for the sheer presence of the man.

He was three or four inches taller than she, about six foot two. She liked tall men; short men made her uncomfortably aware of her height, made her feel graceless and huge. His hair was short, dark and curly, almost black, and his eyes were brown. A pleasant external package, but his most arresting feature was the two-inch jagged scar that slashed past his right eye, a bare half-inch from the socket. Whatever the scar's history, it had very nearly cost him half his sight.

Flustered, she grabbed for her malt, which had been melting while she crawled beneath the desk. She took a hasty gulp, swallowed too fast, and winced as a spike of pain sank into the middle of her forehead. She nearly groaned, caught in the insidious trap that was the ice cream headache.

She realized with a start that he was speaking to her. At her, actually. She took a smaller swallow and almost smiled as the pain started to ease. "Excuse me?" she asked.

He sighed impatiently. "I said, if you'll just hand over the keys, you can be on your way. I'm sure you've got plenty to do. Somewhere else."

Her temper rose in response to his sarcasm. She welcomed the surge of irritation—it lessened the effect of those marvelous brown eyes. "I do not have plenty to do," she said.

He raised an eyebrow at her. "No doubt."

She coughed. "I *mean,* I'm supposed to help you set up. Answer any questions you might have, give you a tour of the facility, and set up the computers. Not toss you the keys and be on my way."

"No?"

"No."

"Too bad." He dropped his briefcase on the desk from about a foot. It hit with a crash and popped open automatically. Stephanie was impressed in spite of herself. "Let's get to it, then. Here's the lease, signed. Here's my list of references. Here's—hold still."

He sighed, pulled out a handkerchief, and leaned forward. Gripping her chin lightly, he started rubbing her forehead with the handkerchief. Stephanie hoped it was clean. At least he didn't spit on it first. "You've got dirt all over your forehead. And ice cream on your skirt. You're not really dressed to be crawling under desks, you know."

"I know. But I was here early and I was bored." In her ears, her voice sounded high and strange. For heaven's sakes, the man was wiping her forehead and she felt as warm as if he were kissing her on the neck. She mentally shook herself. What was the *matter* with her today?

Erik Chambers was having difficulty letting go of the gorgeous blonde in front of him. He'd had a hard enough time finding his tongue when she'd popped up from underneath the desk like some sort of grimy goddess. She was, without a doubt, the most beautiful woman he had ever seen, smeared forehead or no. She was tall—nearly his height—with glorious, golden blonde hair piled on top of her head. A few defiant curls tumbled about her forehead and temples. She was pale—no, not pale—white, her skin the color of cream, and her eyes the color of emeralds. A native, he thought. A born and bred Minnesotan. He'd never seen anyone who had skin that color. Or eyes that clear. Or a forehead so dirty—there.

"There. You're clean." He forced himself to let go of her shoulder. She was so beautiful, she made him feel like a fool. Hell, he *was* a fool. Hadn't Jessica taught him enough hard lessons about women? Did he think he needed to learn a few more? "Let's have the tour."

"Right." She showed him the reception area, his office, the utility room, the break room, the rest rooms and the library. It took about ten minutes and she managed to gobble more than half of her malt during the task. Sir—her guardian, Sir Archibald Chesterson—had been right when he said this favor wouldn't take much of her time. He owned the real estate agency she worked for and Erik was the son of a close friend of his, looking for an office in Minneapolis. She had agreed to show him around because she'd read the *Newsweek* article and been intrigued.

"Everything looks good to me. Tell Sir I'll be renting at least the three months, but won't open the branch until after the new year."

"Right."

"I'll get a branch manager in here over the next few weeks, they'll be able to get things up and running for me." He took another look around the reception area, flipped open the briefcase, and pulled out a check. "That ought to do it—rent for the next six months."

"You don't waste any time, do you? You came here with your mind made up and you hadn't even seen the place."

He raised an eyebrow at the blunt question, liking her for her frankness. "I trust Sir's judgment. He knows what I like. Didn't he tell you? We've known each other a long time."

"He didn't say much about you—but he did tell me he knew you when you were little. I can't imagine you as little."

"How well do you know him?" he asked, not terribly interested, but liking the sound of her voice. It was very smooth—like verbal velvet.

"I've known him for ages. I moved out a while ago, but we still—"

At her words, for some reason, a thwarted jealousy so great he could hardly see swept over him. He felt foolish for not realizing it right away. Obviously, this girl was Sir's mistress. Sir was very handsome and *very* rich and English to boot. Everyone knew women flipped over English aristocrats. And she was the type, too—blonde, leggy, smart, and just ambitious enough to realize the life of luxury one could have as Sir's playmate *du jour*.

"Isn't he a little old for you?" Erik growled.

"Who?"

"Sir! And *you* call him Sir," he sneered. "You don't even know his real name."

Shocked, her green eyes blazed. "I do too! And what do you mean, too old for me? He could be a hundred years older than me and he'd still be perfect."

"Ha! Perfect for rocking by the fire, maybe, but not lovemaking. As I'm sure you've figured out." He watched with interest as the color rose in her cheeks and her eyes widened.

She popped the plastic top off her drink and stepped close. "Five seconds."

"What?"

"To apologize."

"I never apologize." Insults he expected. Shouts, maybe even calculated tears. At the very least, a tantrum. But this deadly calm, this was something new.

The color had faded from her cheeks and she looked horribly pale. Her eyes blazed out at him, narrow and tilted at the ends like a cat's. He began to feel a little ashamed of himself. What was he doing, tormenting this silly thing? He had more important things to do, and besides, she wasn't so bad. Maybe she was very poor, and needed to sleep with Sir so she could pay rent or eat or something. Sure. That was it. That was—

She threw her drink on him, her arm blurring so fast he had barely time to register the fact she'd moved before semi-frozen dairy product smacked him in the face and chest.

"You have a filthy imagination," she said while he coughed and sputtered. "And by the way, Mr. Know-It-All, you forgot to include your security deposit with the rent check." He felt chocolate malted drip down his neck and shirt, to the floor and peered at her with an expression of amazement. He was even more amazed when she ripped his check in two and threw it at him. "Good-bye, Lord Vader. I doubt the loss of your business will send Sir into financial ruin. Certainly it won't bother *me* either way."

She turned and he heard the door shut firmly behind her. He tried to say something, but his head was spinning. "Wait!" he croaked, dabbing ineffectually at his shirt. He couldn't let her go. She was the most amazing creature he had ever met. And he didn't even know her name. "Wait!"

In the hall, Stephanie was resisting the urge to bang her head against the wall. Creep or not, the swine in the other room was the son of her guardian's best friend. Sir had asked her to do this one thing, this one small favor, and she'd responded by ruining the man's suit.

She squared her shoulders and pulled open the door. Erik was trying to mop himself with the two halves of his check. "I'm sorry," she said. "I shouldn't have done that. I really am sorry. But that was an awful thing to say."

"I know," he said. He had said it to upset her, to make her mad or make her cry. Certainly not to drench him! "Wanted to make you mad."

"You did. But I shouldn't have done it anyway. Here, sit down. I'll get some paper towels. God, you're shirt's ruined."

She gently touched his damp chest, biting her lip. "I guess I'll have to get you a new one, I don't think the chocolate stains will ever come out—hey!"

He knew a few tricks of his own and he grabbed her wrist, sat down, and pulled her into his lap. When she had touched his chest, a frown on her usually smiling face, heat had uncoiled in his belly and his mouth had gone dry for the second time in just a few minutes. He suddenly had to touch her, had to have his hands in that glorious hair and his mouth on hers. A mad impulse, one he should definitely struggle against, but he wouldn't. Couldn't.

"Chambers, you grabby schmuck, if you don't let go you're going to get another milkshake in the—mmph!" For heaven's sakes, she thought in stunned amazement. I drenched him and he's *kissing* me? What kind of a disincentive is that?

He plunged his hands into her hair and pressed his mouth to hers in a searing kiss that quite literally took her breath away. His mouth was slanting over hers again and again and she clung to the arms of the chair for dear life, dimly glad they were sitting down because her legs would have never supported her through this. She gasped and he made a funny little groaning sound.

She didn't want to end this, but no matter how much she was enjoying the kiss she could not let it continue. And she certainly was enjoying this. Yes, indeed. He really knew how to kiss. He really—no.

NO!

She shifted her weight and drove her elbow into his groin, not without regret. He groaned and shoved her off his lap. "Aagh, that *hurt* you silly little —"

"Serves you right," she said breathlessly, climbing to her feet. "Sexually harassing the help—and you rich enough and mean enough to know better."

"Harassing, hell," he growled, some of the color coming back into his face. He didn't trust himself to move just yet, but she hadn't put her full weight into the blow, so he didn't feel like throwing up. "You enjoyed it as much as I did. And you're not my employee."

"That is hardly the point," she said primly. She swept her hair back from her face and straightened her jacket. He saw there was ice cream on her blouse. Again, that surge of desire. He fought it down. "Good-bye, Chambers, you lecherous creep. I'm sorry about your suit, even if you did have it coming. Because you're a friend of Sir's, I'm not going to the authorities, though by rights you should be charged with sexual harassment."

"If you did I'd just counter-sue for assault."

"You had it coming and we both know it. Good-bye, Chambers," she said again. For some reason, leaving was difficult. She took a step away from him and then another. She was almost at the door now, yet still reluctant to leave. She looked at him, for what she honestly believed to be the last time, and thought she might weep. He was beautiful and so alone. No one scowled constantly without cause. "Good-bye. I won't be seeing you again, I think." She shut the door firmly and practically ran for her car.

"Wait!" he shouted after her. "What's your *name*?"

Chapter 2

"IT WON'T WORK, Sir," Stephanie announced, kicking off her flats and stretching out on the sofa. There was a roaring fire in the hearth which effectively fought the chill of the old mansion. Even in high summer the house was chilly, and it was late September.

"What won't work?" Sir—Sir Archibald Frederick Chesterson—stood with his back to the fire, smiling and occasionally taking a pull of smoke from his pipe. He looked every inch the English aristocrat he was and Stephanie realized suddenly she had never seen him in anything but a jacket and slacks, or a tuxedo, or a three piece suit. Certainly never in blue jeans or even a robe. Strange, for she had known her guardian since birth, he was closer to her than any father, but she had never seen him in comfortable clothes.

Well, he was rich and titled and old. Maybe he wasn't comfortable unless he was in a suit.

"Child? Are you listening? What won't work?"

"That favor you asked me to do. Erik Chambers. Show him around town? Help him get organized? I won't do it. He's a beast. A lout. A real ass, too—he didn't say a civil word to me all morning and then he insulted me so I threw my drink on him and then I left." She omitted the kiss, flushing even now as she thought of it. She had never been kissed like that before and would never forget it.

"You knew he would be somewhat...difficult to work with," Sir reminded her. Everyone called him Sir. He loathed his first name, believing his mother must have been in a foul mood when she filled out the birth certificate. America wasn't a country for titles, so Sir Chesterton wouldn't do. Mr. Chesterton seemed too common for a man of his background; Sir wore his nobility like a cloak and no one could help but be aware of it. So everyone simply called him Sir and that was just right.

He had never married, and indeed had few close friends, so there was no one to call him Archie (thank heaven). There was no one to call him father, either, but the glorious blonde lying on his couch might as well. "I warned you from the beginning he might be difficult."

"I know, but I didn't know he—" Would be such a great kisser, she had been about to say, but obviously that wouldn't do. "I didn't know he'd be such a creep," she muttered. "And I don't mean to let you down, but the man is so insufferable, I just can't—"

Elsewhere in the great house, a door slammed. Stephanie and Sir both looked around at the sound. Slamming doors weren't a rarity in this house, but it was usually Stephanie doing the slamming. No one else would dare—most of the doors were over a century old and Sir's reverence for all things antiquated was well known.

Rapid footsteps in the hallway. Stephanie sighed and lay down again. She couldn't deny her attraction to Jerkface and she didn't want to disappoint Sir, to whom she owed everything, but all the same it wasn't feasible to expect her to—

"It won't work, Sir," Erik Chambers said, striding into the library. He spotted the older man in his usual spot in front of the fireplace, looking cool and calm. Eric felt a surge of admiration for this man, so like his father in background, so much warmer in personality. He'd known Sir for years, and had mentally adopted him as a sort of distant uncle. Indeed, when he was younger he had fantasized Sir really was a relative.

"What won't work, Erik?" Sir asked, puffing smoke like a benevolent dragon. He did not glance at the couch, but inwardly smiled. Something was coming, and with any luck, he'd get to watch.

"That idiot agent you sent to show me around. She's completely out of control. She assaulted me in my own office and on top of that, she's flighty, undisciplined, and—"

"Undisciplined!" Stephanie shrilled and sat bolt upright on the couch. Erik, ruthless businessman and all-around grouch, blanched and actually took a step backward. "Flighty! Me, out of control? Might I remind you that you insulted my guardian after grumping around the office all morning and as for undisciplined, *you* kissed *me*, remember? You are *such* an ass." She was getting to her feet now, red in the face, lips pressed tightly together. She looked like she was going to launch herself at him. He saw she hadn't changed out of the suit she'd been wearing earlier, she'd obviously come straight from the office to her lover's—

To her lover's —

"He's your guardian?" Erik asked, trying not to let his jaw drop.

"Yes! My guardian! He's my guardian and you're an idiot! Anyone with half a brain could see that, you evil-minded cretin! How could you even suggest that we—"

"Didn't I tell you Stephanie was my ward?" Sir asked, looking as distressed as he ever did, which wasn't very. "I take it there was some sort of misunderstanding. I'm sure we can work everything—"

"Wait 'til you hear what he said," Stephanie said, sitting down again.

Erik sprang into action. He couldn't let her tell Sir of his blunder, even if it had been a natural assumption. Sir most likely wouldn't mind—he was astonishingly easy-going—but there was always a chance that he might. He might and Erik couldn't risk losing face in front of this man.

And why was he so thrilled to hear their relationship was that of father and daughter, rather than mistress and sugar-daddy?

"I need to talk to you." He grabbed her by the arm and hauled her up from the couch. She squawked in anger and tried to pull back, but he was hustling her toward the door, saying over his shoulder, "We'll just be a moment."

The door slammed and Sir was left alone. He chewed on his pipe stem and strained to hear the conversation going on a few feet away. He felt no shame in eavesdropping. It was his house, after all.

"How the hell was I supposed to know he was your guardian?" Erik roared. Sir frowned at the noise. Well, he wouldn't have to wander closer to the door to catch their little chat, anyway.

"It's none of your business *what* he is to me!" his precious darling shrieked back. Sir winced. He'd had Stephanie screeching in his face before and it was most unpleasant. He could almost feel sorry for Erik.

"And what's the big idea, blabbing what happened this afternoon to Sir? Who else did you tell?" Erik had lowered his voice, but it still carried clearly. Stephanie, Sir knew from past experience, would not lower hers for some time. He wondered what the servants were thinking. Surely they could hear her, even in the west wing. They had known Stephanie since babyhood and were probably trying to figure out a way to rescue Erik without incurring their mistress's wrath.

"Blabbing? *Blabbing*? Let me remind you that if you'd kept your hands to yourself there wouldn't have been anything to blab. And if I want to take out a newspaper ad that says, 'Erik Chambers is a filthy-minded pig who can't keep his hands off his real estate agent', that's my business, and if I want to tell Sir what an ass you are, that's my business, too."

"You started it! Throwing your milk shake on me."

"It was not a milk shake," she said with stiff dignity. "It was a chocolate malted with extra chocolate sauce."

A pause, and then a sound that might or might not have been a chuckle. "Extra chocolate sauce?"

"I was tired and needed the sugar rush."

Erik snorted. "That's the last thing you needed, you little hellcat."

"Stop calling me little. I'm almost as big as you are. When you hunch over like that I *am* as big as you are."

"I'm not hunched over."

"Quasimodo had better posture."

Again that sound, as if Erik was choking back laughter. "Quasimodo?"

"Look, why are we wasting time arguing? It's obvious that because you're such a simian wretch we can't work together, so let's just call it quits and—"

"Ah, so you're a quitter, are you? I should have figured. Run into a little opposition and it's run home to daddy. Or Sir, in this case. Probably broke your legs getting here to complain about big, bad, Erik Chambers. How typically female."

"Don't make me go back to the ice cream shop for something else to drench you with."

"Okay, okay, I apologize. And I'm sure you're sorry, too."

"*I* already apologized. Twice."

"Then what are you arguing about?"

"I have no idea." Then, in a small voice Sir had never, ever heard from his ward, she added, "I'm sorry about your suit."

"I had it coming."

"Yes. Yes, you did." The door was thrown open and Stephanie hurried in, Erik on her heels. He looked dazed. She looked triumphant.

"Ah," Sir said. "Did you two work everything out?"

"We'll give it a go, for your sake," she said. "But only because you seem to think it's a good idea."

Sir nodded, inwardly jubilant. "I do, I do." He cut himself off, not daring to say more. It wouldn't do for them to get wind of his plan. "At any rate, I'm glad you two decided to stick with it."

"We have."

"Yeah, and if that's all, I guess I'll be getting home. It's pretty late, and I should have been out of here a couple hours ago." Stephanie went to the closet and fished out her purse. She felt very tired, all at once, and wanted nothing more than a hot shower and bed. It had been an exhausting day. She fumbled for her car keys, her hair falling forward in a gold curtain that hid her face.

"You don't live here?" Erik asked, surprised. He certainly wouldn't have minded living here.

"Of course not. I haven't lived here in years," she replied. That will teach him to think her a child. If he called her 'girl' one more time, she would...

"Two years, to be exact," Sir said. "I remember it well. She moved out on her twenty-first birthday and nothing I could say would persuade her to remain."

Stephanie dropped her purse and ran to him. She threw her arms around him and said, "Sir, darling, don't start. You know I loved living here, and I love you, but I couldn't live on your charity for another minute."

"Charity? Caring for the child of my best friends wasn't charity. If you had lived here until you were older than I am now, it would have made me perfectly happy."

"I know," she said steadily. "That's why I had to leave."

Erik had ceased to exist for Stephanie as she spoke with her guardian. He found that interesting, if a little irritating. She obviously loved Sir a great deal, but that hadn't kept her from leaving the nest and finding her own place in the world. And what a nest! The place was a twenty-room monster, with plenty of space for Sir, Stephanie, and the New England Choir. Three meals a day, extravagant gifts from a doting guardian, love, the instant gratification of her smallest wish—and she had left!

His admiration of her, already quite high, went up another few notches. He knew what it was like to leave wealth and privilege and the only people you had for an uncertain future. It was a difficult choice even if you didn't care for the people living in the house.

"I had to see if I could make it in the Big Bad World all by myself," she said, her arms still around Sir. Erik fought down a stab of jealousy. "You know what it would have been like for me here if I had stayed. 'Darling, did you have a good day at work? Oh, that's right, you don't have to work, I provide for your every need. Well, let's have lunch and then you can go spend several thousand dollars on your spring wardrobe.' I couldn't have stood that much longer."

"It wasn't wrong," Sir said, desperation clear in his voice.

"Of course it wasn't wrong! I had a wonderful childhood and I've got you to thank for it. Does it seem—I mean, it's probably pretty quiet around here, now that I've left, huh?"

"That," he said, "is an understatement."

"Well, look. I've got to get home, but how 'bout I spend the weekend at the house? It's so pretty out here this time of the year, and it would be nice to get away from the city for a couple days."

"That would be wonderful. I'll have Shirl stock up on all your favorites."

"Don't you say a word to Shirl! She'll go on a shopping binge and you won't see her for two days. I'll surprise her Friday night."

"So she can shop all day Saturday to satisfy your gigantic appetite."

"Oh, you! Hush." Stephanie looked wry. "I can't help it if I have a healthy appetite. And look! I really have to go." She slung her purse over one shoulder, gave Sir a good-bye squeeze, and waved her keys carelessly at Erik. "See you tomorrow, boss," she said with a smirk and then was out the door.

Click, click, click of heels on tile and then the front door slammed.

Erik breathed out. The den, which had been cozy and warm seconds ago, now seemed too empty and gloomy. The whole house seemed to loom about them.

"I, for one, can't wait until this weekend," Sir said, but Erik heard the tremor in his voice. Here was a man, Erik thought, who had wealth, title, and just about everything a body could want, but when you stripped away the aristocratic veneer, he was just an old man who lived for his child's visits. And never mind that she was his ward, not of his blood. They were closer than most parents and children he had seen.

"Me, too. My God, this place got dark in a hurry."

"She is all the light in this world," Sir said, still trying to sound casual and uncaring, still not fooling Erik. "My world, anyway. Say— why don't you come for the weekend, too? Lord knows there's plenty of room. And I get tired of rattling around in this mausoleum."

Erik had been waiting for just such an opportunity. He jumped. "That sounds fine. I'll show—say, sometime Friday evening?"

Just as Sir hadn't fooled Erik, so Erik's nonchalant acceptance of his invitation didn't fool Sir. "That would be lovely. And I will too warn Shirl. Two hearty appetites under the same roof all weekend will empty our cupboards unless steps are taken. Immediate steps." He took another pull on his pipe and looked Erik up and down. "You have grown up quite nicely, young man. But then, I always knew you would."

Erik didn't think this had anything to do with anything but he remained polite. "Thank you. Could I have a drink? It's been a long day."

Sir looked horrified. "Of course! What a wretched host I am. Here I've been, babbling on and on, while you've...what would you like?"

"I'll get it." He crossed the room to the small wet bar and fixed himself a Rusty Nail. "So Stephanie's your ward, huh? I didn't know that."

"No, you thought she was my mistress." Sir watched in idle amusement as the blood rushed to Erik's face. "No, no, don't be embarrassed. What else would an old man like me be doing with a creature so fair? In this day and age, it's a natural assumption, but I'm too old for such tricks and I never could abide having a mistress. They're so...so..."

"Money-grubbing," Erik said, a frown creasing his face. His father had several.

Well...not exactly his father. Erik's father had died when he was less than a year old, leaving his mother with a sizable life insurance policy that she made last about five years. When he was six—or, to put it another way, when the money ran out—his mother remarried. She hadn't much choice, she disliked working and despaired at the thought of doing it for another twenty years. Brian Chambers had loads of money. That had been enough for the new Mrs. Chambers. The fact the man hated children, was cold and hateful to both of them, was of minor consequence.

Erik wished he might have known his real father. Surely his blood relative would have been an improvement. His stepfather cared nothing for him or his mother. Erik couldn't understand how his mother could stand living with a man who didn't much like her, who cheated on her with a string of mistresses, who did nothing for her or her son save pay the bills. And yet she remained. In fact, money was apparently all she required of him. Erik had never understood her. "Just money-grubbing morons," Erik said again and, even to his own ears, he sounded spiteful and petulant.

"To be fair, neither you nor I have been anybody's mistress so it's not for us to cast judgment," Sir said with tact. Erik's bitterness toward women was worse than ever, but that was to be expected. As a boy, he had been hurt by his mother, and as a young man, he had been monstrously betrayed by his fiancée. And Lord knew his stepfather was no prize. Sir began to wonder if he had made a mistake, thrusting his ward toward this bitter young man. He had thought Stephanie's kind heart and spirit could surpass any man's prejudices, but perhaps he had been—

"So tell me about Stephanie. When did she come to live with you? Are her parents dead?"

Sir took a deep breath. "Well, that's a long story, Erik. Do you have some time? I warn you because nothing gives me greater joy than discussing my ward, I'm very annoying and time-consuming that way. You do have the time? Excellent." He sat down opposite Erik and set his pipe in the ashtray. "Her parents and I were great friends. I had even dated her mother as a very young man, younger than Stephanie is now, and let me tell you she is the image of her mother—but she has her father's eyes.

"The three of us met at Harvard—her father was my roommate and her mother was my girlfriend. She and I didn't stay together long, as the passions of youth tend to burn out quickly, but we parted amicably and she remained a dear friend. I introduced her—her name was Veronica—to my roommate, whose name was Brian Dares. Americans, both of them, and so fiery! I envied them their passion. English born, I fear most of my passion was bred out of me by the time I was ten. But when I was with the two of them, I could pretend..."

Sir's eyes were looking through Erik and he went from happy to brooding. Erik stirred. It was painful to watch an old man recall long-dead friends. He began to regret staying to pump the man.

Sir smiled and looked at Erik, really looked at him, instead of through him. "Forgive an old man's rambling, son. I haven't thought of Ronnie and Brian in years...since Stephanie moved out, anyway. She is so like her parents, though she never knew them. So fiery and independent and passionate. I see them all over again when I see her and sometimes it hurts. But I digress. I was telling you about Ronnie and Brian. When the three of us got together I could pretend to be fearless like they were—and they were fearless. Stephanie is the same way, to my sorrow. It's not good to never be afraid.

"But anyway...the two of them got along famously, being quite alike, and they married right after they graduated. I was Brian's best man and it was one of the most exciting days of my life. We were all excited; Ronnie and Brian were the first of my friends to marry, so it was quite the do. And Ronnie looked so beautiful, with that blonde hair and that white skin and the dress. She called it the biggest dress in the world, and it did dwarf her a bit." Sir laughed, once again not seeing Erik, only seeing Ronnie as she must have looked that day. "I had even gone shopping with her to help pick it out. Yes, I did. She didn't want Brian to see her in it, but she wanted a man's opinion, so I was elected. Her mother was scandalized, but I was honored. My infatuation for Ronnie had long since faded...I loved her, I wasn't *in* love with her. And so I was delighted to see the two of them together. They were both brilliant, did I tell you? Oh, my yes. Smarter than I, though that's not such a boast."

Sir paused to relight his pipe, walking to the fireplace as he did so.

"Ronnie, especially, was extraordinarily intelligent—she had to be, for a woman to make it all the way through Harvard in that day and age. That's why we broke up, as a matter of fact. Books came first with her, always. Myself, I was a little more easy-going about my studies and never understood why Ronnie couldn't be persuaded to leave the books for a movie or a party or some such thing. But, anyway, I was talking about Brian and Ronnie, not Ronnie and Sir Chesterson."

Erik was hanging on every word. He had expected to be bored out of his mind until Sir got to Stephanie and her entrance in his life, but hearing stories of her long-dead parents was fascinating. It was as if he could know her better by hearing of those who had made her.

"So they married, and settled in Boston, and I went back to England. My father had grown ill and there was much to attend to, the estate and handling the money and such. I stayed there a long time, but came back to America when Brian informed me Ronnie was going to have a baby. A baby! At last! They had been married almost ten years by then, you see, and I wasted no time coming back to Boston. For all Ronnie's vivacity and fearlessness, she had miscarried twice before the third month, but she was in her sixth month now and all looked well." Sir lowered his voice. "They waited until she was six months gone before writing me of the baby. Didn't want me to worry about her more than I was."

Erik nodded. Sir continued. "When I got there I found Veronica was still working; she was an attorney and planned to work until her eighth month. Stuff and nonsense! I made her quit immediately, over her protests—she said they couldn't afford to lose her income, but I had money to spare." For a moment, Sir looked grim. "Always have and for once it came in handy. Anyway, I gave them a check for a grotesque amount and told them to bank the bloody thing. Then I informed Mr. and Mrs. Dares that she was to quit working until after the baby came and I wasn't to hear any more about it. They fought me, of course. Americans are so sensitive about taking money from friends! But I wore them out. Ronnie was too pale, you see, and Brian was working too hard so she could work a few hours less each week. Ha! Enough of that rubbish, that's what *I* said. That friends of mine should be in such dire straits!"

Erik had been fascinated before. Now he was spell-bound. Had he ever seen Sir this upset? Had anyone?

"So Ronnie quit her job. She had to quit, you know. In those days, there was no such thing as maternity leave. She quit her job and fretted about finding another one, but I told her that if nothing else, she could be *my* lawyer. I would have given her an annual salary of six figures without blinking an eye and they knew it. That is how Stephanie is like them—she doesn't like me taking care of her any more than her parents did." Sir laughed without a trace of humor. He went to the wet bar and fixed himself a drink. After several sips, he continued. "Another month went by. Ronnie was looking beautiful now—not so ghastly pale, though her complexion had always been fair—and she had that glow pregnant women sometimes get in their later months. We were having fun again, the three of us, it was just like our college days. I bought them everything I could, over their protests. When they wouldn't take any more money, I'd fill the house with groceries when they were out. Oh, that made them mad, to come home to a fully-stocked refrigerator and freezer! Ronnie would scold me and scold me, telling me I was spending too much and had given them more than enough, but I wasn't repentant. No I was not! Another time I got rid of their old furniture— wretched stuff, falling apart it was—and bought them a living room and dining room set. You should have seen their faces! After that, they were afraid to leave me alone in their home."

Sir laughed, sounding like a child who has played a good joke on those older and wiser than he. "So when they went out, they would take me with them. Ronnie did, mostly—Brian was still working during the day, but sometimes it was the three of us. Mostly they went shopping for baby things, but were afraid to buy much. The money I had given them they were saving until after the baby came. They were very practical that way. So we'd go look at cribs and clothes and such and they'd leave, and I'd give the saleslady my Gold Card number and have them ship to the house whatever it was Ronnie or Brian had their eye on. So after a few days of that, we had a fully stocked nursery—crib, clothes, changing table—everything. Oh, what fun! After that, they were afraid to take me with them, and equally afraid to leave me in the house. Those silly, silly Dares! Brian would try to—you know, talk tough. And Ronnie would scream like a fishwife. 'Sir!' she'd yell. 'If you don't cut it out I'll—I'll—I'll call you Archie!' That was, of course, the worse thing she could come up with, short of denying me their friendship, and they would never have done that. But I just laughed. I was having too much fun to take her threats seriously.

"So a little more time went by, and Ronnie was now in her eighth month and quite fat. Like fools, we thought she was safe. And we were fools. All the—all the gallivanting about town we did, shopping and having fun, when I should have put her in the hospital the minute I got to town. What did the cost matter? I had money to burn. But we—*I* was having too much fun to do that. I—"

Erik knew what was coming had to be bad. The tone in Sir's voice, for one, and Stephanie's parents weren't here, were they? "Stop it. Right now. You couldn't have known."

Sir raised tortured eyes to Erik's face. Erik nearly flinched from the pain and self-recrimination he saw there. "But I should have. I should have! She had miscarried twice before. We thought we were safe because she had never carried a child so long before and we *were* safe, to a point. We worried she might lose the child, we never dreamed the child might lose her."

Sir drained his glass. Immediately poured another. Drained that. Erik was stunned. Never had he seen Sir lose so much of his calm. Never.

"So her water broke, four weeks early. Right after dinner, in fact. Dinner I had put on the table. She got up and took a few steps and suddenly there was a mess, a terrible mess on the floor, amniotic fluid and blood, so much blood...we rushed her to the hospital. Brian nearly killed us on the way there; he had thrown caution to the winds when he got behind the wheel. I sat in the back with her and held her hand...she was still bleeding and we knew that pregnant women don't bleed like pigs when they bring forth life...we thought she was bringing forth death and she was, she was."

Sir set the glass down. His hand shook, so he stuffed both hands in the pockets of his jacket and continued tonelessly, like a man reading aloud *The Wall Street Journal.* "We got to the hospital and they took her away from us, rushed her away and that was the last we saw of her. She was...she was crying hard and trying to hold on to both of our hands and there was blood splashed all over her legs and thighs, making her dress cling, and they made her sit in a wheelchair and wheeled her away, and we tried to follow, and she was crying and calling our names and begging the nurse to slow down so we could keep up, but they didn't listen...they wouldn't let us, and Brian fought them and they knocked him out—they had to give him something because he was as hysterical as she, they made him sleep and put me in the waiting room. I was as upset as Brian but I—they assumed I was calm and in control. And I suppose on the outside, I was. But on the inside, I was screaming as loudly as my poor, dying Ronnie."

Sir's voice was still dry, but his eyes were very bright. "In those days, men weren't allowed in the delivery room, but I think we wouldn't have been allowed to watch the delivery even today, because it was that bad. It was that...bad."

"How long?" Erik asked quietly. "How long did they make you wait by yourself?"

"Not long at all, actually. Two hours and a doctor came out and said, sorry, so sorry, she's dead, but the baby is okay, the baby is fine, the baby is a girl. Brian didn't wake up until the next morning. I wouldn't let them bring him around with a shot. Why hasten his unhappiness? And when he woke he grabbed me—I had been sitting by his bed, holding his daughter. She was tiny and beautiful, and her mother was dead. I loved Stephanie from the moment I laid eyes on her, her with her father's eyes and her mother's hair and both parents' zest for life."

Sir's pipe was out again, but he slammed it down without looking around, and continued his ghastly tale.

"She was all by herself in the nursery, no babies born that week at the hospital. I went to see her an hour after the doctor told me what had happened. I went to look, and there she was, all by herself, and she looked so alone, so I asked if I could hold her, and the nurses were sorry for me, and they allowed it. And I cried *very* hard —my poor Ronnie! All cold and by herself downstairs in the morgue! I cried and woke Baby Girl Dares, but she didn't cry. Just looked at me and grabbed my finger, and that's when I fell in love. So I—well, I asked if I could feed her, because Ronnie wasn't—you know, she had been planning to breast feed, but—well, you know. And I played with her and put her down for her nap and fed her when she woke up, and took her in to see her father when *he* woke up. And he grabbed me, he didn't even see the baby, he grabbed me and lurched up in the bed and shouted, 'Where's Ronnie? Where's my wife?' and I said, Brian, please, she's dead, she died and no one could help her, but they saved the baby, see your tiny daughter, Brian, they saved her, and she's all there is of Ronnie, now."

The old man was trembling like a frightened puppy. Erik went to him, led him to the couch. "You don't have to tell me the rest," he said gently.

"But I must! And I will! I have never told anyone this, not even Stephanie, and it has burned in my breast for twenty-three years." Tears were trickling down Sir's wrinkled cheeks and he trembled still. "I told Brian that his wife was dead and I watched the color drain from his face. I tried to show him his daughter, but he struck at me and he said...he said, 'Get it away from me. That thing killed Ronnie.'"

"Jesus! He didn't."

"He certainly did," Sir said, angry now. "He tried to dash her from my arms, but I held on and backed away from him. You're distraught, I told him. You don't know what you're saying. The baby didn't kill Ronnie, Ronnie died of internal hemorrhaging. 'Shut up, I don't want to hear about Ronnie, and I don't want that thing near me. Get it *away* from me, or I'll crush its skull beneath my foot.'"

"Jesus," Erik said again, feeling sick.

"Yes. It was as awful as you can imagine. A week went by. Ronnie's funeral came and went. They had to send the baby home with me. Brian would have nothing to do with her, so I took her home. Home! Ha! She should have been in a house with her mother and her father. Instead she was in a hotel room with a bachelor who knew nothing about babies, motherless and with a father who hated the sight of her. I tried calling him but he wouldn't answer the phone. I tried talking to him at the funeral but I had the baby with me and he swore to kill her if I brought her near him. I couldn't—I couldn't leave her in the hotel room by herself and Brian wouldn't see me if I had her in my arms. Another week went by. I named the baby Stephanie Veronica Dares. Brian wouldn't fill out the birth certificate. He wouldn't do anything. He wasn't going to work, he wasn't doing anything save sitting in the house going through his and Ronnie's scrapbooks and wedding album. He had dropped fifteen pounds by the time Stephanie was a month old. He was hard and cold...nothing like the carefree friend of my student days. Ronnie was his life, and without her, he was nothing. It was...painful to watch."

"What did you do?"

"What could I do? Brian was making preparations to sell the house. He had already thrown away or sold most of his and Veronica's things. And the nursery! God help me, I don't want to think about what he did to the nursery. Anything that reminded him of Veronica or Stephanie he hated and destroyed. He even made preparations to change his name—Ronnie had been Mrs. Dares and he couldn't bear to be Mr. Dares anymore. Finally I went to him—without the baby, I had found someone to care for her when I went out—and requested custody. He gave it, happily. Signed everything. Said, 'If you must keep it, make sure you keep it away from me.'" Sir shuddered. "Yes, that's exactly what he said. I'll remember it forever, because that was the last time I saw him. I went back to the hotel, packed, and made preparations to go back to England. I, too, wanted no more of the coast, wanted nothing to remind me of Brian and Ronnie.

"Just before I left, I went to Ronnie's grave and told her that I would take care of her daughter forever, that she would want for nothing, and I would love her as if she were my own. And then we left. We didn't come back until my darling was ten, and then we came to Minnesota. I'd never been there, there were no painful memories in the Midwest, and I wanted Stephanie to grow up in the country. And here we've been, for thirteen years."

Erik's breath whooshed out. He'd been holding it for a long time. "That's quite a story. Poor Stephanie. You never told her?"

"Dear God, no! I couldn't tell her. It's such a terrible story. And what good would it do, telling her the truth?"

"No, I suppose you were right. So what happened to Brian? When did he die?"

"Die?" Sir looked ten years older than he had thirty minutes ago and infinitely unhappier. "My dear boy, Brian isn't dead. He's alive and well and living in Boston, and has been for quite some time. In fact, you know him well—he's your stepfather."

Chapter 3

ERIK STUMBLED across the hotel lobby, drunker than he had ever been in his life, save for freshmen week at Boston University. People hurried to get out of his way. No one made a move to remove him, even though this was the Minneapolis Marriott, one of the nicest and most expensive hotels in the area. No one would dare throw him out, no matter how drunk he was, no matter how long he lingered in the lobby. He was too rich.

He fumbled in his pocket for his card key and lurched toward the elevator. The people about to step in abruptly decided they had business elsewhere and in seconds he had the lift to himself.

His mind was still spinning with all that Sir had told him, despite his effort to numb the knowledge with alcohol. His stepfather was Stephanie's father! The man had abandoned that baby girl for a woman he didn't love and a boy he wouldn't love. Now the frequent absences from home could be explained. Now the man's dislike of all children could be understood. Brian Dares Chambers refused to get close to anybody ever again, be it wife or stepson or daughter. Easy to see the reason why.

For the first time in his life, Erik felt sorry for his stepfather, someone he had always disliked and at times, hated. The man had lost everything and, for all his money, had nothing.

Well. He had Stephanie. Not that Stephanie knew that, thank God. If she ever knew that her father abandoned her, that her father wished her dead, why, she would—would—

What?

Erik pondered this as he stumbled down the corridor to his room. The lovely twit was just kind-hearted and stubborn enough to immediately go in search of her father if she learned he was alive, no matter how poorly he had acted at her birth. And then Brian Chambers would blow her out of the water. Hell, he might even try to kill her, as he had when she was a newborn. Erik knew his stepfather as no one else did—no one but Sir—and Brian Chambers was the coldest, most ruthless of men.

Since his wife died, anyway. Before, he had been kind and funny and happy, Sir's dear friend and Ronnie's loving husband, trying again and again with his wife to have a child, and once a child had been conceived, joyously anticipating that child's birth. Erik had trouble picturing the man in such a way, but Sir had known Brian, known him and loved him, and Sir had told Erik. So Erik knew. Knew—what?

Knew just how much trouble Stephanie would have? Knew Stephanie would try to find her father come hell or high water and the one person who could help her was Erik Chambers? Apparently Sir realized he couldn't keep the truth from Stephanie forever, not in good conscience, so he had told Erik and now Erik had to—had to—what?

"What?" he said aloud, fuzzily. Thinking was very hard. He was very drunk, and thinking was coming just awfully slow. He had to sober up and figure this out. Quickly. He had to help Stephanie find her father. Except he was already found. So he had to help her win her father over. Except that would be impossible, the man hated everyone. Except Stephanie was very persistent, and Erik knew that if anyone could win over that tower of ice, it was her. Except she didn't know there was a tower of ice to win over.

"Let me help you with that, Erik," Stephanie said, and now he was sure he had passed out and was dreaming, because the object of his thoughts had plucked the key card from his fingers, opened the door to his room, and pushed him inside.

"You're blitzed," she said, helping him to the bed. "I've been waiting for you."

He clutched her. She was so beautiful. She didn't deserve a father like Brian Chambers. He was so mean, and she was so kind.

"I have come to confess, but I see you're too drunk to understand a word I'm saying, so it'll have to wait until morning," she said, still trying to lug him to the bed.

"I have to confess, too," he said, knowing that Sir wanted him to tell, but not drunk enough to do it. Not nearly drunk enough. "First, I need a drink."

"You've had plenty. You need to lie down. But first you need to let go of me."

"Can't help it. God, you're luscious. Effortlessly luscious, as far as I can figure. How do you do it?"

"I'm not doing anything. Now let go before I drop you." She sounded grim, but he knew she would never do it. She was too kind, too beautiful. His hand sought her breast and she gasped. Then she let go and he crashed to the floor. "Dammit! Will you quit pawing me? Do I need to find you a prostitute?"

"You dropped me!" he cried, lying in stunned rage on the floor.

The floor? Well, there were advantages to be had on the floor...he wriggled around until he was looking up her skirt. Except she wasn't wearing a skirt, she had changed into jeans and a sweater. Curses!

She was laughing as she bent over him. "Oh, you're so drunk and you're going to be so embarrassed tomorrow. Come on." She pulled him into a sitting position and started to drag him toward the bed. He was so cute, lying on the floor, looking at her like a dazed child. As always when she looked at him, her heart turned over and she wondered how it would be to smooth away the frown lines in his brow.

She hauled him to the bed, no mean feat, and helped him sit on the edge. She pulled off his shoes and heard him sigh as he lay back. "Did I tell you that you're the most beautiful woman I've ever seen in my life?" he asked, staring up at the ceiling, which was lazily spinning.

She froze. Dropped his shoes on the floor. Straightened up and looked at him. "You're drunk," she said again, sharpness lending brittle edges to her voice.

He sat up at the tone of her voice, clutching his head and groaning. "I sure am," he said. "But that doesn't change the fact that you're drop-dead gorgeous. And why are you so funny about it, anyway?"

"No one—I mean, Sir has—but he's like my father, he has to say things like that."

He looked at her for a very long time. Her face burned. He was being kind to her, kind and complimentary, and she must remember that and not take it so seriously when—

"Stephanie, you little idiot—"

"I'm not little," she said automatically.

"—listen to me." He leaned forward and grasped her hands. Turned them up. Kissed her palms. His eyes were bloodshot, but kind. "You are the most beautiful woman I've ever seen in my life. And I've seen a lot of beautiful women. You are also the first woman I've ever seen who doesn't give a flying fig about my money. You are also the first woman I've ever seen who isn't afraid of me. You are also the first woman I've ever seen who thinks of others first. You are also the first woman I've ever seen who—did I say you weren't afraid of me?"

"Yes." She was smiling, but her face was still red. Her hair was down and it gleamed gold in the room's dim light. He reached out to touch it.

"You're also the first woman I've seen who hasn't chopped all her hair off, or permed it to death, or moussed it to death. It's just there. It's nice. In fact, as your client, I forbid you to touch it in any way chemical. Don't go near it with scissors, or let anyone near it."

"You're not really my client. That's what I came to tell you. This whole agency thing is—"

"Tomorrow," he said. "We'll talk about it tomorrow. We'll spend the whole day together and we'll iron everything out."

"The whole day?"

"Yes. We'll go fishing. You can take me fishing. Do you know how?"

"Yes. Joe—Shirl's husband—started taking me when I was little. I know where we can catch some fat brook trout."

She never ceased to amaze him. She was perfect in every way. Beauty, brains, personality, and she could fish. God was too kind. He sighed and dropped her hands.

"You're right. Tomorrow I will be hideously embarrassed that I told you all these things, but I'll worry about that tomorrow. Except— you must promise not to use what I've told you against me."

"What?"

"Promise." He was deadly serious, she could see that, and she fought down the hurt. He didn't know her, they'd only met that morning, and she had to give him a chance to realize she wasn't like most of the women he had known.

"I promise never, ever to use anything you've told me tonight against you," she said, raising a hand.

"Good, thank you," he said, and passed out.

She turned his legs around so he was lying on the bed, covered him up, and kissed him on the forehead. She tried to smooth out the lines in his forehead but they wouldn't go. Even in his sleep he frowned.

Smiling, she went to the desk and left him a note, then left, quietly shutting the door behind her.

In the morning, Erik woke with a raging headache, but knew from past experience that a few aspirin would take care of that. It was all the hangover he ever had.

He gulped down aspirin with three glasses of water, then stripped and hit the shower. He was knotting the belt of his robe when he passed the desk and saw Stephanie's note, and last evening's activities came back to him with a thud.

Erik—you were awfully drunk last night, I hope you're feeling all right this morning. You proposed we'd go fishing and I'm going to take you up on it—I'll meet you in your room at 9:00 a.m.. Don't worry about gear, I've got everything we'll need. If you're not feeling up to it, no problem, we'll do it another time.

Stephanie.

"Fishing!" he said aloud, crumpling the note. Then he relaxed his fist and tried to smooth out the wrinkles in the note so he could read it again. Absently, he touched her signature. "Fishing! We can't go fishing. We've got an office to run. We've got—hmmm." He was the boss, he could go fishing whenever he wanted. And the machine would catch all the phone calls—assuming there were any, which wasn't likely. The office wouldn't be open for business until the new year. And—why not? He could look at her all day, see the sun shining on her hair, hear her laugh. He would pretend total ignorance and she would teach him how to fish. It would be...fun?

"Hmmm," he said again, and started to dress.

At 8:45, there was a knock on the door, and he heard her say, "Knock, knock!" He was ready by then, had, in fact, been waiting for her for half an hour, and he crossed the room to open the door. She stepped across the threshold and he burst into laughter.

Disgruntled, she wrinkled her nose at him. "We're going fishing, not dancing," she said. She was wearing an old, cream-colored sweatshirt with the logo, "Come Along Quietly", faded blue jeans out at the knees, and her hair was tied back with an old green scarf. "I almost couldn't get up here, I look so awful."

He pulled her to him in a rough, almost embarrassed hug. God, he was glad to see her!—then made himself let go. "You look adorable," he said. "And that sweatshirt is perfect for you. Good morning."

"Well! Thank you, and I'm glad to see you're a morning person. Though I sure couldn't tell yesterday. Feeling okay? You were pretty blotto last night"

"How nice of you to notice and immediately bring it up. And I'm fine. Just a headache. Want to get going?"

"Sure. I've got all the stuff we need in the car, you just need to bring your bad old self along."

"Well, my bad old self is ready. Lead on."

He followed her out the door, thinking, today I have to tell her that her father is alive, that I know who he is and he wants nothing to do with her. Jesus! No wonder Sir held off and held off. How am I going to do this to her?

Somehow, he would have to find a way.

Chapter 4

"OKAY, HERE'S THE plan. We can't let our shadows fall on the water or it'll scare the fish away. They're really skittish in this part of the creek."

"Why don't we go to another part of the creek, then?" he asked, reasonably enough.

"Shhh! Not so loud. We have to earn the fish, that's why. It hardly counts unless we work for them. Besides, the really big ones are in this stretch. Now follow me and stay low."

She crept across the meadow, hunched so low she was nearly crawling. He followed her, trying not to grin. He'd never seen her so intent. Certainly she'd never been this quiet before.

"And watch out for the cows," she muttered.

Cows? Erik looked around doubtfully and spotted three bovines placidly grazing about twenty yards away. Watch out for them? What were they going to do, besides make messes? He mentally shrugged and bent lower, keeping behind Stephanie as she crept closer and closer to the edge of the creek.

One of the cows looked up from its grazing and snorted softly. Stephanie stiffened at the sound, and began backpedaling immediately. She ran into Erik, who had stood still when he saw her starting backward.

"Let's go," she muttered.

"My lucky day," he murmured back, tightening his grip around her waist. Then he nearly fell over when he saw all three—All three? All *three*? –cows begin to gallop toward them, mooing menacingly.

"Run!" Stephanie shrieked, turning in his arms and shoving him. He stumbled backward, then turned and started sprinting toward the barbed wire fence which now seemed about ten miles away. Behind him, the galloping grew louder. Erik lengthened his strides. Stephanie passed him on the right and actually reached the fence a full five seconds before he did. She scrambled underneath, limber as an adder, and then bent to hold the wires so he could crawl through.

He roared, "Move back!" Startled, she did so, stepping back so quickly she tripped and fell over. He braced himself on the wooden post and vaulted over, sailing past her and landing in a flexed crouch.

There was an angry snort and he turned to see the cows milling about on the other side of the fence, glaring at him with bovine dislike. Then, as one, they began trotting away.

"Holy God!" Erik choked, breathing hard. "We could have been trampled!"

"All's well that ends well," Stephanie said, standing up and brushing herself off. "Nice jump, by the way." The scarf had fallen out of her hair and she bent to pick it up, chuckling. "Actually, we didn't do too badly. We almost reached the bank that time."

"Almost—you mean you knew about the cows?"

"Sure. I've never actually fished this part of the creek. But I always try. One of these days the farmer will leave them in the barn and then we won't be able to count all the trout we'll catch." Her eyes gleamed. She was obviously picturing a creel full of brook trout.

He stared. "You brought me here to be...trampled?"

"Oh, heck no!" She smiled at him, her eyes sparkling mischievously. "I brought you here to gauge your stamina. You have a great stride and that jump was truly spectacular. I judge all my fishing partners by the same ruler."

He shook his head and bit back laughter. "You really meant it when you said we had to earn the fish."

"Of course I did. It'd hardly be fair, otherwise." She tied her hair back and picked up pole and creel. "C'mon, let's get back to the truck. We'll swing around to the south end and see if we can't pick up a few brookies before lunch."

"I just melt when you talk about fishing," he murmured, picking up his own pole and following her up the hill. "Now talk about hunting. Go on. Torment me."

"Ha. Ha. I have laughed. Race you to the truck, old man." She broke into a trot, looking over her shoulder and grinning at him.

"Old man!" he cried. "I'm not even thirty yet! And I remind you," he went on, lengthening his stride until he was pacing her, "that I was right behind you all the way to the fence."

"Oh, yeah," she jeered. "The operative word being behind."

He grabbed for her. She swiped at him with her pole. In such fashion, they reached the truck.

On the way to another part of Hay Creek, she asked him about the scar. He knew it was coming; people always asked about it. Stephanie had held out longer than most, which surprised him. He hadn't thought patience was one of her virtues.

"I was mugged," he said.

"You're kidding! What'd they do, try to steal your eye?"

"There were four of them and one of me, and one of them had a broken beer bottle and did a little bit of Christmas carving."

Shocked. "You're kidding."

Sour. "Yeah. I am kidding. I tell that to all the nosy parkers who ask about it."

She nearly drove off the road. As it was, after a startled swerve she hit the brakes and pulled over, put the truck in park, and faced him. "Okay, spill it. What happened?"

"Fly fishing. My casts are a bit—wild at times. Managed to drag a hook across my face."

It was at this point that women would coo platitudes and ooh over the scar. He waited, resigned.

She laughed. He stared at her. She laughed harder, clapping a hand over her mouth. "I'm so sorry," she giggled around her palm. "It's not funny at all. It's just—it's an interesting mental picture, that's all. Oooh, I bet you were pissed."

He shrugged. He hadn't been pissed. Once the doctor had stitched him up, he hadn't cared one way or another. The women who paraded through his life had never minded. Or, if they had, they had been too infatuated with his wealth to say anything.

She quit laughing. "I am sorry, Erik. It's not funny. Don't mind me, I laugh at some dumb things."

"No argument on this end. Don't worry about it. Yours was a unique reaction. No one's ever laughed at my being scarred for life before. Congrats."

She made a face and put the truck in gear. "I said I was sorry. Besides, it's all for the best."

"Oh?" He couldn't wait to hear this one. No one had ever said it was for the best.

"Well, I happen to think the scar gives your face tremendous character. Really! You've got a great face," she said with the frankness he was beginning to find quite pleasant. "And there's such a thing as being too perfect. You'd probably be just another pretty boy without the scar—your basic flat-faced magazine model. *Bor*-ing. With it, you look like you've been places. I like it."

He was mystified and tremendously flattered. He hoped it didn't show. "Thank you. I have never been complimented on my scar before."

"First time for everything, big guy," she said, and pulled into traffic.

Chapter 5

"I THINK SIR'S playing matchmaker," she said. She tossed out a beautiful cast which dropped her lure six inches from the far bank.

He wished he hadn't told her the truth about his scar—that a sloppy cast had nearly taken out his eye. She was one of the most skilled anglers he'd ever fished with and he'd worked with pros. She instinctively knew where to stop and cast, her casts all went exactly where she wanted them to go, and she kept pace with him through hilly, brambly country without complaint. It was embarrassing, especially since he wasn't nearly as skilled as she was.

Still, he enjoyed fishing, always had. What better way for him to get out of the house for hours at a time as a boy? And it was nice to be with someone who loved the sport as he did, who didn't mind sitting on a bank for two hours waiting for a strike, who didn't think twice about plowing through some brambles to reach a choice pool.

Not that she was waiting very long between bites. Stephanie's creel was nearly full. He had caught three small brook trout, all in the last hour. Amazingly, he didn't mind. Well...he minded a little. It would have been nice to limit out, as she was close to doing. But for the most part, he had fun with her and already hoped they could go fishing again soon. One by one, she was shattering his long-held ideas about women. It was exhilarating, if a little disconcerting.

"Matchmaker, huh?"

"He does that once in a while. Tries to fix me up with someone," she was saying. "He wants grandchildren."

"I know," he answered. He casually aped her effortless cast and sent his lure into the bushes on the opposite bank. "Dammit!"

"Easy, Erik. You're casting too hard. No wonder you carved yourself up."

"Oh, shut up."

"I don't want you to get mad or anything," she continued as if he had said nothing, "but I thought you ought to know what he's been up to." She got a bite and set the hook. In about thirty seconds she had landed another eight-inch rainbow trout.

"Nice one," he said. She handed him the fish. By mutual agreement, he had cleaned them all. She knew how to do it, she had explained to him. She just didn't like to get fish guts under her nails. He had told her he didn't mind fish guts under his nails, so he would do it on the condition that she would have dinner with him that night. She had agreed.

"Don't get mad at Sir, either," she said. "He cares for you a lot and he apparently thinks we'd make a good couple. Of course, he has no idea how jaded and bitter you are about women."

"Why are you telling me this?" he asked. He chose to ignore her jibe and tossed the newly-cleaned trout into her already-bulging creel. He rinsed his hands in the creek and dried them on his pants, then sat back on his heels and waited.

She had been tying on a new lure, studiously not looking in his direction, but now she put both lure and pole down and squinted at him.

"Well—I felt bad about tricking you. I mean, I knew what Sir was up to, asking me to show you the office. He's got a dozen agents who can do that. But he asked me, so right away I knew something was up. And you've got a bad enough opinion about women without thinking I'm trying to trap you, too."

"So you're not trying to trap me, huh?"

"Uh-uh." She picked up the lure and began fussing with the knot again. Was she trying to trap him? Absolutely not. Was she curious about spending more time with him? Oh, yes.

"Want to go to bed with me anyway?"

She nearly dropped the lure. Her painful embarrassment on the subject of their mutual attraction was a mystery to him. Still, he liked seeing evidence of her innocence. He hadn't known there were women left in the world who could blush.

"No, I do not!" she cried, making the knot in her line bigger and bigger. By now it was nearly the size of a walnut. "Need I remind you that I can—and will—defend myself against inappropriate action?"

"What is that, some kind of threat? There isn't a malt shop within twenty miles, and besides, you couldn't defend yourself against an inappropriate insect bite, and if I want to—hey!"

She pushed him over. Balanced on his heels as he was, he went into the creek without any problem at all.

Although Minnesota had enjoyed a warm summer, it was nearly the end of September and the creek was chilly. Erik, now soaked and freezing, sat up, spluttering and spitting out ice cold water.

Stephanie was leaning over the bank. "Cut that out. You'll scare the fish."

"That's it," he said, not sure if he wanted to laugh like a loon or strangle her. He started splashing toward the bank. "You're going in on your head."

"I wouldn't," she said primly, backing up. "Those old bones will probably snap like kindling."

"I'm only twenty-nine!" he howled, grabbing for her, yearning to feel her neck between his fingers.

"Oh, jeez, you're older than I thought. Better get out of those wet clothes before you catch pneumonia," she teased.

"Misery loves company," he said. He grabbed her by the arms but she moved back and, to his surprise, flipped him with a deft martial arts move. He knew a thing or two about judo himself, and simply held on. When she had completed the move, he merely yanked and now it was her butt in the dirt.

"Uh-oh," she said conversationally.

"Better hold your breath," he warned and flipped her into the creek.

She came up with a shriek of outrage, spitting out water. Her enraged splutterings were completely unintelligible. He ignored her and held out a hand. She grabbed it and tried to pull him back in, but he had been expecting such a move and was braced. "Quit fooling around and get out of there. And get that pouty look off your face. I told you I was going to toss you in and I did. Need I remind you that you started it?"

"Drop dead," she muttered, shaking her head like a dog. He stepped back to avoid the spray of droplets.

"Thank you, no. Well, this has certainly been an exciting day but I think that'll be it for fishing, hmmm? We've probably scared the trout into hibernation. Let's go get dinner, I'm starving."

There was a long silence. Erik assumed she was seething. He kept a wary eye on her. "Trout don't hibernate," she said. She was not looking in his direction. "I'll have to go home and change."

"Me, too. C'mon, let's hit the trail."

They picked up their creels, tackle boxes, and poles, every step a squish, both trying not to notice the other's grin. Stephanie had to choke off a giggle more than once, and Erik was gritting his teeth to keep looking grim. It really was kind of funny—the two of them looking like drenched cats, occasionally glaring or hissing at each other, while at the same time giving the other a wide berth.

"Oh, and Stephanie?"

"What?"

"I'm delighted you're not trying to trap me."

Obviously, she was supposed to be bowled over by this earth-shaking statement. Ha! "That makes two of us," she said. Then stopped, confused. He had taken the news that her presence in his life had been a lie with nary a blink. Indeed, it was as if he had been expecting it. "You're not mad? About Sir and me fooling you?"

"Nope."

"Why not?"

"Sir sort of spilled the beans last night."

"Oh. Well, I'm not surprised. He hates deception and I'm not too fond of it myself, despite what you must think. But he only had your best interests at heart. He really likes you," she added. He was warmed by her loyalty to the man, "I'm sure it seemed like a good idea at the time. You did like the office and you'll be around for a couple months, running it."

"No, I won't. Don't you remember? I'm getting a branch manager in to do that for me. I'll be heading back to Boston soon. I just came out here to say hello to Sir and give the place a once-over."

She was gaping at him. He came around the side of the truck and picked up her fishing pole. He wondered what the problem was.

"You—what? You're going back when?"

"Pretty soon. Within days."

"Oh," she said in a very small voice and climbed into the cab. He was left standing there for a moment, then shrugged mentally and went around to the passenger side.

She didn't say another word until they reached her apartment.

Chapter 6

"I'LL JUST BE a minute," she said shortly as she pulled up to her apartment complex. "You can come in if you like."

Without a word, he got out and followed her inside. Stephanie wished he would go away. She was trying very hard not to cry and she was horribly afraid she wasn't going to succeed. And she was furious because she had to try at all. What was she getting so upset about, anyway? So he was leaving soon? Big deal! She'd only known the jerk for two days, she ought to be happy to bid him *adieu*.

But for some awful reason, she felt like she was going to be ill. Had felt like that the minute he said he was finished up here. So quickly! She hadn't counted on that; she'd assumed he be around a few weeks, getting things set up. She had been so happy that he'd taken the news of her deception with such grace. Maybe they could have gotten something started. Most likely not, but he seemed so wonderful she had fun pretending. He was a few years older and probably a lot more sophisticated than she was, and certainly she must seem like the worst sort of child to him, but he had been kind to her, he tolerated her tantrums, he thought she was beautiful, and she had been looking forward to the next few weeks with uncharacteristic longing.

And then, of course, there was the small fact that her knees turned to water whenever he came anywhere near her.

"Nice place," Erik said, more to break the silence than anything else. She had been completely silent the whole way home, which he knew meant trouble. Whether for him or for someone else, he didn't know, but he didn't like it.

He'd gotten through the first half of his confession. Somehow he had to tell her the second half—that Sir had tricked her, too, that Erik's reason for being in Minnesota had less to do with the branch and trial than either one of them could have imagined.

He didn't like her silence. She was a non-stop chatterbox with an opinion about everything. He liked that about her, liked that she never hesitated to say what she thought. When she was quiet it gave him the creeps. "You've done a great job—this place has you all over it."

"Thanks," she said. She stepped aside to let him in. "I'll change my clothes and we can be out of here."

"Okay. Can I have a towel?"

A ghost of a smile appeared. "Sure. You're still pretty soaked."

"You, too, blondie," he said good-naturedly, catching the towel she tossed his way.

"When do you think you'll be leaving?" she asked casually, peeling off her sweatshirt and tossing it in the general direction of what he assume was the bathroom. He noticed her clean laundry was in neat piles on the coffee table. She bent to pick out a bra and panties and he politely looked elsewhere.

"End of the week, I suppose. Definitely by Saturday."

"Oh. Do you need a ride to the airport?"

Actually, she'd most likely be going with him to Boston, only she didn't know it yet. "No, I don't think—" he began, turning to look at her, then choked the rest off. He realized with a shock felt all the way to his toes that he could see the outlines of her breasts through her wet t-shirt. Rational thought ground to a halt. He tried to swallow and couldn't.

He must have made some small sound for she asked with concern, "Are you all right?"

"I will be in about thirty seconds," he said grimly, crossing the room in two strides and seizing her by the arms. "God! You're so beautiful. I've been watching you all damn day and I can't figure it out—how in the world can you be so beautiful and so *good*?"

Her puzzled, "Huh?" was swallowed as he kissed her, his mouth pressed to hers as he drank of her but could not get his fill. He dimly realized he would never be full of her, never, and didn't know if that was a good thing or a terrible thing.

Her arms came around him and held tightly. His hands had been cupping her face, but now they slipped down and found her sweet, high breasts. A shudder racked her frame as he hands slipped up her t-shirt and settled on the cool flesh.

A groan as he rubbed his thumbs over her nipples. He didn't know which one of them had made the sound. Probably him. God, she felt so soft, so sweet. So—cold and clammy.

"Time to get you out of these clothes," he murmured against her mouth. "Which is what I've wanted to do since I first laid eyes on you."

"Not bloody likely," she murmured back. Or tried to. What actually came out was, "You're an amazing kisser."

"I haven't even gotten started." He peeled her t-shirt off and raked his gaze over her. Her arms were marbled with gooseflesh, but that didn't hide the flawless beauty of her skin, the impudent, pink nipples that thrust out and up, her long, graceful neck. Her neck. How had he never noticed what a pretty neck she had? It cried out for diamonds. No—emeralds. With those eyes, definitely emeralds.

"I'm going to buy you an emerald necklace," he murmured, pressing his lips to her throat. "Right away. Is there a decent jeweler in this town?"

She shivered delicately. "Before or after I die of pneumonia?" Startled, he looked at her. Really looked. She sounded so aloof...almost disinterested. "C'mon, Erik, let go. I'm freezing."

Stung, he let her go. She grabbed a clean sweater from the coffee table. "I'll be right out. Stay put." She hurried from the room, clutching the sweater to her front, her shoulders hunched.

Erik tried not to feel hurt. She moved him so how could she remain calm when they touched? Didn't she like him? Maybe his scar repulsed her. Well, that wasn't the case. Not with Stephanie. She liked his scar, God knew why. Maybe she just wasn't interested. Hell, she hadn't even been interested in the necklace. Maybe that would change once the necklace in question was around her neck. Sure it would. Women couldn't resist pretty baubles, especially expensive ones. Stephanie wasn't like all the others, but in this she would be the same.

She'd be grateful for the fine gift. And then he'd find out once and for all what it would be like to possess that glorious body.

He grabbed the Yellow Pages and began thumbing through the J's.

In the bedroom, Stephanie was shaking like a leaf. She had sunk to the floor and was rocking back and forth, shivering. Her body throbbed with need. One kiss and she had been ready to let him have her on the living room floor. What was it about that man? He thought women were a nuisance, but called her beautiful and good. Claimed they were only after a man's money, then offered her jewels. Painted himself as an emotionless businessman, then tossed her in a creek. And for a woman-hater, he could send reason flying with just a few kisses. Obviously while discovering women couldn't be trusted, he had sampled more than a few.

He turned her inside out and that was before laying a hand on her. When he actually did touch her—oh, God!

And now he was leaving. After captivating her, infuriating her, and whetting her appetite for more, he was going to vanish as suddenly as he appeared, going back to his woman-hating, wheeling-dealing life.

She hated him.

A rap on her door. "Steph? Okay if I use your phone? I'll get us a reservation somewhere."

"Fine." Her voice was deceptively calm. "I'll be out in a minute." She made herself stand and walk to her closet. No use crying over spilt milk. And it was especially useless to mourn missed opportunities. There had been nothing between them, so there was nothing to get upset about.

Near tears and furious to be crying over the man, she yanked a dress out of her closet and made herself concentrate on getting ready.

In the living room, Erik was ordering jewelry. "Look, just send your biggest emerald necklace to the Minneapolis Marriott, name of Erik Chambers. I don't care what it looks like, just so it's big. I want emeralds the size of robin's eggs, got it? No, this isn't a joke, you small-town moron! Call the Marriott if you don't—hello? Hello? Damn!" He slammed the phone down. Idiots! He could hardly woo Stephanie with baubles if he couldn't produce the goods. Minneapolis might think it was a big city but it was no better than a ghost town if it didn't recognize a legitimate customer when one picked up the phone.

Maybe buying her dinner would be enough...no, no, not for his Stephanie. Most women, sure. Hell, a Big Mac and a Coke and they would be his for the night. But Stephanie would require extra persuasion. Prime rib and champagne, at the very least.

Erik began to pace the small living room. He had broken CEOs, he had demolished corporations, he had held out against the trappings of marriage-hungry debutantes. He could figure out the blonde. The key was deducing what she wanted, offering it to her for a price, and collecting his prize. So think, dammit. What did she want?

Jewelry? Maybe. A good shot, anyway, but one that was unlikely to pan out, given the lateness of the hour and his urgent need to have her tonight. This very evening. He'd only known her for two days but she was driving him crazy, both physically and mentally. He had to have her and quickly. He suspected that would be the only way to get her out of his system.

Money? Again, a possibility—but for Sir. Her guardian had more money than any three millionaires; she had been surrounded by luxury and had wanted for nothing her entire life. She might not—scratch that, she definitely wouldn't be impressed with his money. Hadn't she been unmoved by his wealth from day one? Heck, she probably had more money than he did, when you got right down to it. Certainly Sir had a sizable trust fund hidden away for her somewhere and she was sure to inherit the man's considerable fortune upon his unfortunate demise. So forget money.

What did she like? Well, she was a damned good fisherman. Fisherwoman. Whatever. Solid gold lures? Maybe. He could buy her a bait shop. A possibility, but it lacked romantic appeal. "Stephanie, as a token of my esteem, as a bargaining chip to get you into my bed, allow me to present this bait shop, fully stocked with nightcrawlers, suckers, leeches, and minnows, for your fishing pleasure." No, no, no.

Think about her. Think about her. What was she like? Ummm...smart. Funny. Noisy. Opinionated. Kind. Kind?

Kind, kind, kind. Heart of gold, that one. So what if he promised to donate a few thousand to a soup kitchen or a hospital, in return for an evening of carnal pleasure?

Oooh. Oooh. Good idea. Great idea! She wouldn't be able to resist that one. A night with him, and in return hundreds would benefit, including him.

Now—how much? At least a hundred grand. Hmmmm—maybe he could build a new wing at Mt. Sinai hospital. Hell, he'd give the city half a million to build a free clinic or a couple of soup kitchens or something. That ought to knock 'em dead.

A tiny voice in the back of his mind tried to point out Stephanie could donate at least that much herself, and didn't have to sleep with him to accomplish it, but he made it shut up, fast.

Chapter 7

"YOU LOOK BEAUTIFUL. As always."

"You're very kind. A rarity."

They were walking along Nicollet Mall after having dinner at the top of the IDS tower. In spite of herself, Stephanie was having a wonderful time. The restaurant had boasted a view of half the city and the food had been exquisite. She'd had two appetizers, soup, salad, an entree, two desserts, and coffee. Erik had been amazed.

"I can pay for myself if this is going to be too pricey," she'd said with her mouth full. She grinned and scooped up another forkful of linguini. "You're not the only one around here with money."

"No, it's not a problem," he said, grinning back at her. "Slow down, will you? Nobody's going to take it away from you. Waiter? Could you bring over a few more napkins for my dinner companion? Thanks. Be careful, Steph. It'd be a shame to spill on such a pretty dress."

"I'm being carefu—oops!"

After dinner, he had suggested they walk along Nicollet Mall and talk. She agreed, feeling the need for some exercise after such a magnificent dinner, as well as wishing to delay their goodbye as long as possible. So here they were, looking deceptively loving to passers-by. He had put an arm around her waist. She had let him, and so they walked.

"Thanks again for dinner. It was great."

"How could you tell? You didn't wait long enough to taste everything. Whoosh! And it was gone. It was like watching a vacuum cleaner in a red dress. Oof! Don't poke, I'm an old man, remember?"

"You're only five years older than I am, remember?"

"But what I've learned in those five years; you're still a baby."

"In your case, it's not so great, being around a couple years longer. All you've learned are the bad things," Stephanie said soberly. "I don't know what happened to you before you came out here, but somebody was pretty mean to you. Or a lot of somebodies were. And don't deny it, because I know it's true."

He was silent. A little surprised at how well she knew him, and adding up all the somebodies. Stephanie's father. His mother. His fiancée. His business partners. His— "Part of the territory," he said. "Comes with trying to make it big before age thirty. It's not a big deal."

She stopped. "It is a big deal," she hissed, turning to face him. He had to fight down an urge to step back from the naked anger on her face. "Don't you dare make light of it. I could strangle some of those women who've ruined you. I—"

She cut herself off and looked away. He reached out, smoothed a golden lock back, cupped her chin. Her eyes were blazing, nearly snapping sparks. He realized with a start that she was trembling.

"You what?" he asked gently.

Her eyes were no longer angry. Now they were wide, filled with misery. "I wouldn't be mean to you. I think you're wonderful. I know you don't believe me."

He was silent for a moment, holding her, thrilled to his very being that she cared. Finally, he cleared his throat and smiled. "By an amazing coincidence, I think the same thing about you. And I believe you because you always tell the truth. Except," he teased, "when you're masquerading as my real estate agent."

Some of the anger left her face and he was glad to see it go. He kissed her, a quick touch on her sweet, sweet lips. He liked it so much he kissed her again. And again. Slowly, leisurely, until they were both leaning against each other under the street lamps and people passed around them on both sides, smiling.

"I do believe you're the first real person I've ever known," he said, not a little amazed.

"What about Sir?" she murmured, leaning against him.

"He's too cliched to be real. Does it bother him, do you suppose, being a stereotype? How many pipe-smoking, impeccably dressed, richer-than-God aristocrats can there be, outside of novels?"

She appeared to consider for a long moment. "I don't know a one. Maybe if you kissed me again my memory would improve."

"Doubtful," he said, but complied. It might not jog her memory, but it certainly couldn't hurt. "Mmmmm. You taste nice. Like—"

"Like that chocolate cake I had for dessert," she giggled, snuggling closer to him. They were nuzzling on Nicollet Mall in front of dozens and dozens of people. Neither of them cared.

"What a horrendous thought. I was going to say, like flowers and honey."

"Have you eaten many flowers, Erik? Is that how you—don't tickle!"

She shrieked and writhed away from him, but he held her tightly and stole another kiss. "I love you," he said, smiling, and then went cold and released her, quickly.

Stephanie gaped at him, her mouth hanging open. He seized her by the arm and began pulling her up the street, toward their parking ramp. He felt ill. As a matter of fact, he felt like he might throw up. As a further matter of fact, he felt like he had a big mouth and should shut up, probably for the rest of his life.

"You love me?" she panted, trying to match his furious pace. "You love me?"

"Shut up," he growled, furious with himself, furious with her. "Slip of the tongue. Caught up in the moment." And those green eyes. "Shut up. Shut up. It didn't mean anything." She was so beautiful, so kind. He loved her. Would love her, until death did them part—and maybe even after that. He should marry her, and quickly, before some other idiot figured out what a prize she was and snapped her up. "Will you stop talking?"

"I haven't said anything!" she protested. Miraculously, she wasn't screaming at him yet.

Miraculous, hell. He wanted her screaming at him, he wanted her so mad she couldn't see straight. He wanted her to forget the treacherous slip of the tongue that had given her power over him forever. How could he have betrayed himself? How could he have told her the truth? And how could he feel this way about her, about anyone? For God's sake, they'd only known each other two days!

"Did you mean it?" she asked. She seemed stunned. "How could you mean it? We don't even know each other. You don't like anybody, except maybe Sir. And then only a little bit. Are you feeling okay? Erik—Erik! Slow down and answer me! Did you mean it?"

She planted her feet, refusing to be dragged another inch. He swung around to look at her. She looked fresh and young and terribly, terribly hopeful. She was clutching at him, unconsciously tugging at his sleeve.

She was the most beautiful creature he had ever seen in his life.

He loved her.

He refused to believe it. "I told you I love you because you're a leggy blonde and I wanted you in my bed tonight." He shrugged carelessly. "That's why I took you out to dinner. I would have had you and left for Boston tomorrow. And I would have la-a-a-u-ghed all the way home."

He smiled at her. His heart was breaking. He had crushed his beloved out of fear, out of self-preservation. He had built walls around his heart at a tender age, no one could ever come in. He would see to it. Had seen to it.

Now, Erik thought sickly. Now comes the tears and rage. Now comes the right hook.

She laughed at him. "Coward! Scared yourself good, didn't you? Had to try and fix that little slip of the tongue, and quickly, huh? Can't tell the girl you have feelings, God, no. That would ruin everything." She laughed and laughed, holding her belly.

He had never been more stunned in his life, not even when she threw ice cream on him after he accused her of sleeping with Sir. She wasn't going to take the bait and walk out of his life in a rage. He was trapped!

His mouth fell open as he tried to think of terrible things to say to her. His soul felt as if it were on the outside, naked and shrieking for the world to see. He had to get it on the inside, hidden from sight, back where it belonged, and quickly.

She thumped a finger into his chest. "Well, I've got news for you, jerk. I love you, too. Ha! What do you think of that?" She stomped on his foot. "There! That's for being a jerk and a coward. I'll say it again. I LOVE YOU. Eye-ell-oh-vee-ee-why-oh-you." She stepped back and withered him with a glare. "Now deal with it."

Stephanie spun on her heel, head high, and began walking away, very fast. She was so excited, it was all she could do to keep from skipping down the street. He loved her! He loved her! She wanted to cry. She wanted to laugh. She wanted to punch him for being afraid. She wanted to kiss him and hold him in her arms until he wasn't afraid anymore. "You love me, you love me," she sang, not looking back. "Ha, ha, you love me."

From behind her, an anguished howl. "I do not!"

"You love me, you love me..."

"Stop it! Shut up! It's not true! I'm in lust with you, that's what I meant to say." She heard rapid footsteps as Erik ran after her. "I lust you! I lust you! That's all!"

"And we'll get married and have two adorable blonde children. Do you think we could get a Black Lab? I love Black Labs."

"Will you stop? We're not getting married. I don't love you. I'll never love you."

"Do you like kids? I hope we have a girl first. Girls are a lot less trouble, don't you think?"

He caught up with her, panting. "Please—I don't want to hurt you. I don't. But I don't love you. It was a mistake. I didn't mean it."

She smiled at him, a dazzlingly sweet smile. "Why, Erik! For someone who doesn't love me you're being awfully careful with my feelings. What a sweetie you are. Don't worry, I'll give you time to get used to the idea."

"I'm married."

"You're a liar," she said kindly. "A cowardly liar. You should be ashamed of yourself, being so afraid." She put her arms around him and held him as she had longed to do since their first meeting. He stood stiffly within her embrace. "I will never hurt you. I will never leave you. And if anyone does try to hurt you, I'll kick their butts. Did Sir tell you I have black belts in aikido and judo?"

"No," he said, feeling as though he were strangling. "But it explains a lot."

"He let me study anything I wanted when I was growing up. The martial arts interested me a great deal. So did target shooting. Did I tell you I broke the state record for silhouette shooting with a .44 magnum?"

"No." Briefly, he considered recruiting her for his security team. "I don't doubt it, though." She was so beautiful, she would be his secret weapon. That way, she could be with him in Boston and he could see her all the—no. No!

Enough of this garbage. Enough. Enough. He had started out the evening wanting to get her in his bed. Sadly, that want had not changed, instead it had grown to a desire to get her into his life, forever. He would not have it. He had to finish this and quickly.

"Your father's alive," he said calmly. "Your mother died giving birth to you, your father swore never to see you again and gave you to Sir when you were a month old. Sir raised you and kept the truth from you ever since."

She stiffened against him. "You're still lying," she said. "But they're getting less believable. You should be ashamed of yourself. You'll do anything to get off the hook but I won't—"

"Your father's name isn't Dares anymore. He changed it to Chambers. He came out East, made a fortune, married my mother, raised me. Are you getting this? Your father is my stepfather. That's why Sir brought me out here to meet you. Not to look at office space. He hoped I would tell you the truth, because he couldn't bear keeping it from you anymore. He tricked you and he's been lying to you ever since you were born."

For a moment, she stood still as stone, her mouth open, her face a blank as the impact of his words hit home. "My father—my father's alive?" she gasped, staggering a little. He reached out an arm to steady her. "And Sir knew? Has known, since I was born? Sir knew?"

"You bet, babe. What do you think of that? Pretty sneaky, huh?"

"You're a bastard and I'm sorry I told you I loved you," she said. Her voice was the coldest thing he had ever heard. "How long have you known? When did Sir tell you?" She grabbed him by the lapels and yanked him forward. "How long have you been keeping this from me?"

He smiled lazily at her and cupped a breast through her coat. "I've known since last night. I thought I'd leave you a note in the morning. Then you and Sir could have it out and I'd be long g—"

She slapped him so hard, he lost his balance and fell backward onto the pavement. Even as he hit the ground, he was surprised she'd slapped him instead of dealing real damage, as a black belt certainly could have. Before he could recover his wits, or think about what that meant, Stephanie fished his keys out of his sport jacket and ran down the street, crying as if her heart would break.

In truth, it already had.

Chapter 8

SOMEWHERE IN the great house, a door was thrown open. A shout of pure rage echoed in the hallway and steps pounded toward the den.

In his chair beside the fireplace, Sir winced. He put down his book, picked up his pipe, and moved to the mantel, his back to the door. He looked at his reflection for a moment in the mirror and wasn't pleased with what he saw. A tired old man looked back at him, a man haunted by the ghosts of his past, a man who was afraid of his ward as she thundered and screamed down the passage toward him. Not that she would physically harm him. Oh, if only! He would prefer that to the damage she could wreak. She could walk out of his life forever and he'd take a month of traction and eating through a tube before he'd take having to say goodbye to the daughter of his heart.

The door was thrown open and Stephanie's rage blazed out at him, lighting up the room.

"You son of a bitch!" she cried, slamming the door shut behind her. "You knew. You knew, damn you!"

He said nothing. She advanced, white with anger, green eyes eating up her face. "Why didn't you tell me? Why did you tell *him*? How could you lie to me all those years? All those years, my whole life! My father is alive and you never said a word. And when you did tell someone, it wasn't me. It was my father's stepson, that low-down slimy snake! Did you tell him to seduce me, to soften me up, then lower the boom? Did you?"

Sir groaned, shook his head, held his hands up to placate her. This was worse than he could ever have imagined. And what was this about seduction? What had Erik done before telling her the truth?

"You lied! You've been lying to me since I first asked where my father was. Why? Why?" She surged forward, knocking a three-hundred-year-old end table out of her way with a blow of her deceptively small fist. She stopped in the middle of the room, perhaps unwilling to get any closer to him. "Oh, Sir, how could you?" she cried, and then did the thing that, above all, he couldn't have borne. She put her hands up to her face and sobbed.

Given a choice, he would have preferred a broken leg. He hurried forward, his face wet with sweat and his own tears and she hurled herself into his arms as he approached. "Stephanie, please, please don't," he begged, holding her close. "Please, darling child, please don't cry. You know I can't bear it when you cry. Why don't you hit me instead? It'll make you feel better. Only—not in the face, if you please."

"I hate you. I really, really do. I'll never forgive you," she sobbed, snuggling more firmly into his embrace. "And I left Erik in the street."

"Never mind," he soothed, inwardly wincing. "Knowing him, he said something terrible and you lost your temper."

"Well, yes," she admitted, sniffling. She leaned away from him and wiped her face. "He was hateful, just hateful. He's lucky I didn't break his leg. Why did you tell him and not me? He's horrible!" She burst into fresh tears.

Sir thought he might start crying again if she didn't stop. He couldn't bear to see her so desperately unhappy. "Please don't," he murmured, stroking her golden hair. "Please stop. I'll give you a million dollars if you stop crying." Her wails grew louder. "Two million," he amended hastily. "Five million. Please, Stephanie, you're breaking my heart."

"And the worst of it is, I know why you didn't, for all my shouts to the contrary," she sniffed, winding down. "All these years you've been telling me my father and mother loved me very much and asked you to take me before they died. But my father is still alive. He didn't want me." She stopped and wiped her face with the back hand, then took a deep breath and said quietly, "He didn't love me."

Agony sliced through Sir, sharper than any knife. "Stephanie, that's not true. He does love you. He just—he just doesn't know it yet."

"You chose to give me pleasant fiction instead of telling me the truth. I—I'm glad you wanted to protect me. But Sir—why did you wait so long? Why didn't you tell me when I was old enough to understand?"

Sir shook his head, put a hand to his forehead. "I couldn't. I started to a hundred times. I—his actions hurt me so very badly when you were born. The death of your mother—and your father's grief—and you, a tiny baby in need of someone to love you and take care of you. I gladly took you home with me, raised you as my own child, but when the time came to tell you the truth...I couldn't do it. I couldn't bear to—to—" He took her by the shoulders and, in his agony, he had regained the strength of his middle years as he tightened his grip. "Please, please forgive my weakness. Please. I love you more than my life. I have tried to be strong. But I'm an old man, a weak, foolish, stupid old man and I have never been strong, never." He bowed his head and wept. "Not when my poor Ronnie needed me. Not when Brian lost his mind. Not when you needed the truth. Brian and Veronica were always the strong ones, so I never had to be. And now...it's too late."

And Stephanie, who moments before had screamed and raged at this man, held and soothed him as best she could.

Much later, when both were spent, she asked forgiveness for her display of temper. "I was more mad at Erik than at you," she confessed, "and since he wasn't around to yell at, I took it out on you. And the thing is, I knew the whole time I was screeching at you why you hadn't told me. I knew the truth had to be bad."

He nodded mutely.

"But I'm a big girl now, Sir, and I want the truth. All of it."

He nodded tiredly and told her the entire story, starting with his and Ronnie's college days, ending with him keeping tabs on Brian Chambers over the years. Knowing when he married and took a wife. Seeking out the stepson, befriending him and loving him as Sir knew Brian could not.

"Does my father know you and Erik get along so well?"

Sir shook his head ruefully. His hair, usually so carefully coifed, flopped untidily on his forehead. He pushed it back with a sigh. "Brian and I only met once after Ronnie's death and that was brought about by me. I went to see him at his office when I was in Boston for business. You were four or five, I think. It went badly. He couldn't bear the sight of me—and why not? He couldn't look at me without remembering his disgraceful conduct after the death of his wife. He ordered me out, and on my way back to the street I ran into young Erik. He was—oh, about ten. He'd heard his stepfather's outburst and sensed in me a kindred spirit. Anyone his stepfather didn't like, the boy no doubt reasoned, couldn't be all bad. And so we got to know each other."

"I still think you should have told me instead of him, you big chicken."

Sir hung his head. "I know. I saw my chance when he decided to come out here to set up the Minneapolis branch. I thought, I can get the two of them together and he can help her find her father. No one knows Brian Dares Chambers better than myself...or his stepson."

"Too bad Erik's such a loser," Stephanie said rudely, burning inside as she recalled she was in love with this particular loser. "Your plan would have worked, except he only wants to get me into bed..."

"Stephanie!"

"...and I think he's a complete jerk."

"Oh, *I'm* a jerk? You've got some nerve, Stephanie Dares!"

Both turned at the shout. A livid Erik Chambers was standing in the library doorway. His formerly-spotless white shirt was a smeared ruin, his hair was rumpled, his twelve hundred dollar slacks were out at the knees.

Sir gasped. "Good heavens! What happened to you?"

"What happened to me was your wretched ward attacked me, left me for dead, and I was easy prey to muggers until I got up."

"You look awful," Stephanie said sweetly. "Nice shiner, by the way."

"Don't you talk to me. I tell you an unpleasant truth about dear old Dad and you whale all over me! You're not supposed to shoot the messenger."

"That's not why you got slapped and you know it," Stephanie said coldly. "I got a little carried away because we were having such a nice time and ended up saying something I didn't mean, because you said something *you* obviously didn't mean.. You had to take it as a threat to your personal safety and tried to emotionally annihilate me."

She was shocked at the relief on his face. Shocked and hurt. "You didn't mean it? You don't love me? You were just—uh—swept away by the moment?"

She stood very straight and lied through her teeth. Putting all the scorn into her tone she could, she snarled, "Love you? Love *you*? Of course I was kidding, imbecile! I don't even know you! And why would I fall in love with someone who would try to hurt me if I ever— *ever*—was so foolish as to let my real feelings show? You're a wretch, Erik Chambers, a selfish, spoiled, ruthless, cowardly wretch and I couldn't love you if you were nice to me until the end of my days."

"Well, thank God for that," Erik muttered, flopping into a nearby couch. He ran a hand through his thoroughly rumpled hair and grinned at her. "Had a bad moment there. Thanks for setting me straight. We won't go into your numerous character flaws at this time."

"And you can forget about having sex with me," she continued, oblivious to Sir's shocked gasp and Erik's reddening face. "I wouldn't sleep with you if someone held a gun to my head. Good night."

She strode toward the door, turned, and said to Sir, "By the way, I don't hate you for telling him and not me. Your only crime was bad judgment."

The door shuddered in its frame as she slammed it behind her, hot tears spilling down her face. Sir's crime was her own, but forgiving herself was a harder pill to swallow. Hadn't Erik warned her he was no good? Hadn't he told her again and again that women couldn't be trusted? He had indicated in dozens of ways he could never care for a woman. Did she listen to his good advice? No.

Would she listen to her own, the small internal voice that was screeching at her to forget he ever lived? No.

"Damn, oh damn," she whispered and hurried down the hallway. It had been an exhausting night. She was so numb with shock she could barely think. The fact that her father was alive was just that to her—a fact. It didn't stir anything in her. She was aching over Erik, smarting from his words in the street and crying over the look on his face when she told him she hadn't meant it. She couldn't think about her father now, or about Sir and his lifelong deception.

In a moment she came out of her headlong rush and realized she was right outside the door to her old room. Instinct or habit had guided her footsteps and she stepped gratefully into the sanctuary. She had always been happy here, secure in the knowledge that, though her parents were dead, they had loved her very much, that Sir had wanted and loved her, that men didn't lie and everything turned out all right in the end.

Her room was exactly as she had left it. Cream colored walls, rich purple carpet. Her favorite color, though Sir had always told her green was the color that made her shine. Her stuffed animals were waiting for her in the window seat. There was the double bed in the corner with a hand-made quilt her grandmother had made. Sir had taken only two things from Brian Dares, both with his blessing. One of them had been his daughter. The other had been his wife's favorite possession, a quilt her mother had made for her when she was a tiny baby herself.

It was probably the only thing my father didn't wreck, Stephanie realized with her new-found knowledge. Sir said he went berserk and trashed the house. I wonder how he rescued the quilt from my father?

She went to the bed, sat on it, then stretched out, stroking the quilt and staring at the ceiling. Her father was alive. And she was in love with his stepson—no, no, best not to think of that now. Think about Brian Dares. Brian Chambers, actually. He lived. Had lived, all these years, trying to forget she ever existed.

He thinks I killed my mother in my coming, Stephanie thought unhappily. And he's right. But am I to be held responsible for Mama's death? I didn't mean to kill her. Maybe I was too big and she was too small. I'll have to ask Sir exactly how she—no, I really don't want to know. It's enough to know that I'm here and she's not, and that was reason enough for my father to deny my existence.

Sorrow for this father she had never met welled up in her. Her own problems were temporarily forgotten as she empathized with Brian Dares. He had given up everything that reminded him of his dead wife and had lost much more than he realized. She began crying again, more for this faceless father than for herself, and for a mother she had never known.

Thirty minutes later, Erik was standing over her bed, watching her unhappily. Her face was still wet with tears, her usually-smiling mouth drawn down in a sorrowful bow. She hiccupped once or twice in her sleep, as if in some far-off dreamworld she was still sobbing.

Erik thought he might cry, too, if she didn't smile at him soon. And why should she do that? He had brought her nothing but grief.

He cleared his throat. The sound was very loud in this still, small room. In the bed, Stephanie slumbered on.

"I love you," he said quietly. "I'm sorry I made you cry. I think you're beautiful and good, have I told you this before? I want you to be my wife. I want to go to sleep with you every night and wake up with you every morning. I love you. Stop me if you've heard this before. I-" He trailed off, feeling cowardly and tongue-tied. It was all very well to tell Stephanie the truth about his feelings when she was deeply asleep and couldn't hear him, but what about when she was awake? And what was the matter with him, anyway? Why this gut-wrenching fear when he thought of how deeply his true feelings ran? Stephanie wasn't like his mother, or any of the other women in his life. And she couldn't do anything to him that hadn't been done before. So what was the problem?

The problem, he thought grimly, was that Erik Chambers, multi-millionaire and eater of corporations, was a lily-livered coward where Stephanie Dares was concerned. He was afraid of this vibrant blonde, afraid of what she meant to him and what he may or may not mean to her, and to the kind of commitment that might lead to.

"I love you," he said again and was comforted because he was at long last telling her the truth, even if she wasn't awake to hear it.

He smoothed her hair back with his hand and, bending down, kissed her tear-stained cheek. He thought a moment, then circled around to the foot of the bed, pulled her shoes off and unfolded the quilt lying at the foot of the bed.

Stephanie sighed in her sleep and rolled over on her side, hiccuping again. After a moment of hesitation, he got into bed with her, pulling the quilt over them both and switching off the bedside lamp.

As exhausted by the day as she, he was almost immediately asleep, and so didn't hear Sir steal quietly away. The old man had not meant to eavesdrop, coming to check on Stephanie as he always had when she lived in this house, but had stopped outside the door when he heard Erik's declaration of love. Stunned, open-mouthed, he heard everything and then crept back the way he had come.

Perhaps, perhaps, he thought. Perhaps this hasn't been a complete shambles after all.

Chapter 9

STEPHANIE CAME awake slowly, as if swimming toward the surface from ocean depths. She was very warm and almost sinfully comfortable, despite the fact she was sleeping with all her clothes on, on top of the covers. In her room, the dark had always been kind and she felt better for the hour or two she had been asleep.

Wait, now. What was this? She wasn't on top of the covers. She was—someone had pulled a quilt over her as she slept. Probably Sir, coming in to check on her like he had when she was a little girl. He must have taken her shoes off as—as—

Someone was—Erik was in bed with her.

She squeaked and tried to sit up. His arm was across her middle, though, and it was like trying to shrug off a two-by-four. She poked him in the ribs and hissed, "Erik! What are you doing here? Get out of my bed!"

He muttered in his sleep and pulled her closer. She found herself in a tight embrace, her breasts pressed against his chest, her head tucked under his chin. She felt she must protest this, but couldn't remember why. She was so comfortable. And he smelled wonderful. And what was he doing here, anyway? This house had plenty of bedrooms. He certainly didn't have to seek hers out.

"Erik," she whispered again, poking him in the stomach.

"Go to sleep," he muttered into her hair.

She wriggled against him and poked him again. "Erik, what are you doing here?"

He tightened his grip on her. "Stop moving around and go to sleep," he said gruffly. "We can resume our fight in the morning. You can tell me how you can't stand the sight of me and what a jerk I am. I'll agree wholeheartedly. In the morning. As for right now, if you don't quit wiggling your delicious bod I'm going to make love to it. So lie still and go to sleep or you'll have your hands full."

Stephanie became still as stone. My, she wondered. The man was perpetually aroused when he was around women, wasn't he? Maybe, she thought. Maybe he cares about me a little. Enough to—to want me and to come and stay with me in the dark.

"Good night," she whispered into his neck.

"Good night, sweetheart," he murmured back, dropping a kiss on the top of her head and giving her a quick squeeze.

Well. Maybe loving him wasn't such a God-awful stupid thing to do, Stephanie thought. She tried hard to remember that she was furious with him. As she spiraled back down into sleep she promised herself to be mad at him in the morning.

"Hey, sleepyhead. Steph? Wake up!"

Only a minute or two had gone by since he told her to go back to sleep, what was with the man? Stephanie opened her eyes and immediately shut them against the sunlight streaming through the bay window.

"Morning already?" she muttered, rolling away from the light. It was no good, sunlight was splashed all over the room.

A hand gripped her by the waist and rolled her back. Erik kissed her soundly and smacked her on the behind. "Wake up, wake up— come on, I had you pegged for a morning person. You're so disgustingly cheerful the rest of the time. Will you open your eyes? God, it's like talking to one of the living dead." He kissed her again, a loud smack.

She fought him off and staggered in the direction of the bathroom. "L'me 'lone," she mumbled, shutting the bathroom door. A glance in the mirror confirmed her worst fears; she looked a fright, worse than any member of the living dead. "Oh, God," she moaned and started ripping a brush through her hair.

Erik heard her moan and smothered a grin. He'd awakened with absurdly high spirits and for once he knew why. Waking up with that blonde head on his shoulder had started his day off right. What was worse, he couldn't imagine not waking up with her, though until yesterday he'd done so every day of his life.

What's wrong with me? he wondered. Good God, I love her. I love her! How could I have let this happen? And I can't even tell her because I'm such a coward. Not that it would do any good at this stage of the game. His brow darkened as he remembered Stephanie wanted nothing to do with him, now or ever. He'd made it abundantly clear to her that she was nothing but a physical toy to him and she took him at his word.

Erik's good spirits faded and disappeared. With a muffled curse, he threw the quilt back and strode from the room.

Twenty minutes later, a transformed Stephanie emerged from the bathroom. "All right, I'm up, are you happy? Erik?" She looked around the room and shrugged, then crossed to the closet and pulled a tote bag from its depths. She was going to Boston today, no matter what Sir said, and she'd need a change of clothes. Maybe two or three, if she and her father hit it off and he asked her to stay a day or two.

She fought down the ripple of apprehension that moved through her at the thought of meeting this man and started to pack. Never mind the fact that he never wanted to see her, that he blamed her for the death of his wife. Things would work out. She would make them work out.

Finished packing, she found Sir and Erik in the dining room, sitting down to breakfast. She joined them, smiling at the cook who set down a plate of her favorites—fried eggs, ham, hash browns, a big glass of chocolate milk. She realized she was starving and fell to the meal with a will.

Erik, picking the shell off his boiled egg, looked at her plate and shuddered.

"Um eeng oo onton on ii oo ommp eee," Stephanie said, pointing her fork at Sir and chewing furiously. She gestured meaningfully to the tote bag sitting at the bottom of the steps, its sides fairly bulging with clothes.

"What?" Erik said, moodily salting his egg.

"She said she's going to Boston and I can't stop her," Sir replied mildly, looking at Stephanie over the top of his glasses. "As a matter of fact, I've already booked you on this morning's flight. Darryl will drive you to the airport when you've finished eating."

"I'll drive her," Erik muttered.

"I mean, Erik will drive you."

"Frankly, I don't think I can stomach being so close to you during the hour drive to the airport," Stephanie said coldly. The effect was marred by her chocolate milk mustache.

Erik's temper rose to the occasion. Not only was he in love with this silly twit, not only would he never tell her, but she was going to meet his stepfather today, which would be an unpleasant experience for everyone. "Oh, yeah? Well, you sure didn't mind being close to me last—"

"Erik!" Stephanie shrieked, her face flooding with color. Sir pretended not to notice.

"I'm taking you to the airport. Then I'm getting on the plane with you. Then I'm driving you to Brian's office, if you want to see him right away."

"Why?"

Yeah, why? Here was a chance to be rid of her. To never see her again. Ever. Again. "Look. I know this man better than anyone alive...except maybe Sir. You're going to need my help. And I'm happy to give it."

"I won't pay the price for your...kindness."

Now Erik was flushing. "Forget about it. I want to make up for last night. I—" He glanced at Sir, who appeared to be engrossed in his breakfast. Stephanie was watching him with surprise. "Last night. After dinner. I was cruel. I'm sorry."

Stephanie's green eyes went very wide. She clutched at her chest and toppled from her chair, thrashing about on the floor like a landed trout. "My heart!" she gasped. "It can't take the shock! Graaggh!"

He pretended to aim a kick at her hip. "Get up, you're not funny."

She jumped to her feet and kissed his cheek with a loud smack. "I appreciate the help. I've never been to Boston; I wouldn't know the first thing about getting around in that city. And I accept your apology."

"Perhaps Erik can show you some sights," Sir said, not looking up from his breakfast.

"He'll probably be too busy," Stephanie said. "He runs his own company, you know."

Ha! I *am* the company, Erik thought. I guess I can take a day or two off. Or three or four.

"Well, you'll be leaving soon. I wish you the best of luck, dear heart." Sir rose and Stephanie put her arms around him. "If you like, I will come with you."

"No, thank you." She squeezed him tightly for a moment. The moment stretched out as Stephanie seemed reluctant to let him go. Sir wondered if he might faint. At the last second, she dropped her arms and he gasped for breath. "Erik will help me find him. The rest I have to do by myself. And Sir—last night, with all the excitement and everything..."

Erik abruptly got to his feet, sensing Stephanie's desire for privacy. "I'll be in the other room," he said, then hurried out.

"...well, I never got the chance to tell you how happy I am, and how lucky I am, that you decided to take me off my father's hands."

"Oh, now, that's not—"

"Let me finish! Dammit, you just can't take a compliment, can you? You told me that my mother and father asked you to be my guardian before they died, but that wasn't true, was it? What really happened was that my mother died having me, my father lost his marbles roughly two seconds after he found out his wife was dead, and you stepped in to give me a home. I—that was very kind. More than kind. Generous. And I never thanked you. So thank you."

"You're welcome," he said softly.

"And no matter what happens in Boston," she went on, "I will never, ever forget what you've done for me. Ever. Got that?"

"Yes."

"Good. Goodbye." She kissed him and hurried out, stopping only to grab her tote bag, forgetting her half-eaten breakfast. She turned and waved. Somewhat bemused, he waved back. And as the front doors slammed and engines roared, he told himself things had worked out for the best, despite his cowardice, despite the disastrous way Stephanie had discovered the truth. And he could not help feel that a circle, long broken, was now closing. Twenty-three years ago, Stephanie's father had walked out on her. Now, she was walking back to him.

Sir was suddenly very glad she had refused his offer to tag along.

Outside, Erik and Stephanie were climbing into his rental car. Erik's bags were already in the back, as he had packed the night before, planning to leave for the airport from Stephanie's apartment. Things had not, he thought wryly, turned out exactly according to plan. Oh, he was heading to the airport, all right, but not in the frame of mind he expected.

"I never asked you," Stephanie said, buckling her seatbelt as he backed the car out of the drive. "How did you get back here? I took the car, remember?"

"Of course I remember. It was ten hours ago. I called a cab, if you must know. Luckily, I managed to hang on to my wallet during the scuffle so I actually had money to pay the cabbie. Damned muggers. Good thing I came to in time."

"Yes, that was a good thing," Stephanie said seriously.

"You haven't apologized for slapping me," he reminded her.

"That's right. I haven't."

Frowning, he drove them to the airport.

Chapter 10

"DO YOU WANT to go see him right away?" Erik asked, as if Stephanie hadn't bitten two nails ragged, spilled her drink in his lap, and shrieked every time the plane hit some turbulence. The flight attendants were giving her more and more apprehensive glances, especially as the plane was due to land in ten minutes.

Stephanie looked away from the window, where she had been watching the approach to Boston. Her face was very pale. Her eyes were enormous.

A little disconcerted as always by her direct gaze, he plunged ahead. "Because if you wanted to get some rest, maybe clean up a little or something, we could do that instead. If you wanted. I mean, we don't have to race over to see him the second we land."

"Okay," she said, and turned back to the window.

"Okay," he said, relieved. The longer he could put the family reunion off, the better. "Actually, we could have a good time, all things considered. I think you'll like Boston." He made a mental note to take her to his favorite restaurant and to the beach. Might as well have a little fun before her father annihilated her. "We'll be on the ground in no time, hon."

"I've flown before, Erik."

Could have fooled me, he thought, but said nothing. And when her hand crept into his as they landed, he squeezed gently and smiled at her.

She didn't smile back, just got to her feet as the plane taxied to a stop and grabbed her carry-all. He was right behind her as she went up the ramp into Logan airport, then stopped in confusion and said, "Where to?"

"This way," he said, and in a little less than twenty minutes they had their luggage and were getting in the back seat of a taxi. For all its bad reputation, Logan was actually a pretty organized place, once you got used to it, and he was. "Back Bay, 1251 Comm Ave," he told the driver and settled in for the thirty-minute drive.

Stephanie came to life a little then, looking out the window and asking him about certain buildings that caught her eye. It was mid-morning, just past rush hour, so traffic wasn't too horrible. It was a crisp, fall day and Boston had never looked so good to him. Perhaps it was the company.

"You know what the trouble with Minnesota is?" she asked out of the blue, craning her neck to watch a three hundred year-old building fade from sight. "No old buildings. I mean, there's stuff here that was here before the Constitution. So old that our grandfathers' grandfathers' grandfathers walked around in them. Don't you think that's amazing?"

"If you think Boston's old, you should go see Rome. Or Athens."

"Yeah, I guess," she said thoughtfully and went back to gazing out the cab window. "About the oldest thing in Minnesota is Sir. And even he's not that old. It's nice to be in a place that has a sense of history."

"I could take you, if you—we're here. Get out," he said, handing the driver a fifty and waiting for change. He had been about to offer to take her to Rome, of all places. Christ, he fumed, either love her or hate her but make up your damned mind!

"This is Back Bay," he told her. "Probably one of the nicest neighborhoods in the city." He handed the cabbie a ten after the man had hauled their bags out of the trunk. "Thanks, fella. Come on, Steph, follow me."

He led her into his apartment building, past the doorman whose eyes bulged appreciatively at the sight of Stephanie in a red sweater and cream slacks, into the elevator. "My penthouse is on the top floor," he said, despising the way his voice sounded...like he was trying to impress her or something.

"Most penthouses are," was her dry reply. "So. You live in 'one of the nicest neighborhoods in the city', huh?" She grinned at him. Something loosened in his chest at the sight of that grin, which had been mostly absent the last few hours. "Modesty, thy name is not Erik Chambers."

"If you've got it, flaunt it," he leered, backing her into a corner of the elevator. She swung her suitcase out—lightly, he'd give her that much—and rapped him on the knee. "All right, all right, I get the picture. Look, but don't touch."

"I'd rather you didn't look, either," she said saucily, stepping out of the elevator with her nose in the air and turning down the wrong corridor.

"This way," he sighed, jerking his head toward the other end of the hall.

"Oh. Right."

He used his key card and let them both in, turning in surprise at

Stephanie's gasp.

"Oh, wow! Erik, this is so pretty!"

He tried to look at it with her eyes, to see what she was seeing. True, it was the nicest—and biggest—apartment in the complex, costing him five thousand dollars a month in rent. Two bathrooms, three bedrooms and an office, a spacious kitchen that seemed small compared with the dining and living area...the best that money could buy.

Still, he'd never thought of it as pretty.

"You like it? Good. You'll be staying here for...well, as long as you need to."

She dropped her suitcase. On his toe, but he only bit his lip and moved his foot back. "Here? Forget it, jerk, I'm not—"

"Will you relax? I just thought it'd be easier for both of us if we were in the same place while you were in town. My intentions are motivated out of laziness, not lust."

"If you're lying, I will kick your butt."

"Why do you always think the worst of me?" he complained, then mentally shook himself. What kind of an idiot question was that? He wanted her to think the worst of him.

"Why do you always give me cause?" Good heavens, he'd sounded so forlorn. Stephanie felt the first stirrings of guilt. He had been terribly sweet to her ever since they woke up together this morning. And he certainly didn't have to help her find her father. Nor did he need to put her up in his apartment. He could have scribbled his stepfather's address down for her and walked out of her life. "I mean— I'm sorry. I'm tired. That's why I sound like such a shrew. You're being so nice and all I've been doing is grumping around."

"Yes, but nobody can grump and look beautiful like you can, so chin up. You've had cause to be gloomy." He paused, started to say something else, changed his mind. "Come on, I'll show you your room."

He'd called her beautiful again. And the look in his eyes when he'd said it made her knees weak. As she followed him toward the back of the penthouse, she realized she had never in her life felt so frightened, furious, happy, or excited as she had these last three days. And the week wasn't over yet.

"Once you're settled, I thought we might go snag some dinner. Like seafood?"

"Oh, sure. You bet! Seafood's one of my favorite things. I don't have it very much in Minnesota."

Erik grinned. "I ordered the seafood special out there and they brought me fish sticks." When Stephanie smiled back, he added, "I'll take you to Legal's, they'll show you what real seafood is. Let's plan on getting out of here in about an hour, all right?"

"When can we go see my father?" Stephanie asked, as if that was a small item on their itinerary, one of not much consequence.

"Whenever you want. You can stay here as long as you like, so I guess you can see Brian whenever you like."

Stephanie made her eyes get very big and round. "For free?" she asked with sarcastic breathlessness. Then, suspiciously, "Why are you being so nice to me?"

"Well, you have to have sex with me twice a night—just kidding," he added hastily, seeing her look around for something to throw. "Of course, for free. Don't make me out to be a bigger jerk than I am. I might steal a few kisses, but that's the extent of my lustful intent, I swear."

Stephanie hoped he would steal more than a few kisses. A dozen or so would suit her fine. He was a marvelous kisser. Then she thought of all the other women he must have kissed to get so experienced and had to crush a wave of jealousy that startled her. Never mind, never mind, she scolded herself. He's with you now, helping out and being a dear and just try to hold your temper for two minutes, all right?

"Tomorrow, then," she said to Erik's back. "We'll go see him tomorrow. Tonight I want to have fun."

"Well, then, tonight you will," he replied, and went to make dinner reservations for two.

Chapter 11

"JEEZ, ERIK, I feel like I should open a greenhouse," Stephanie complained as he thrust two dozen roses in her arms. They were a beautiful mixed lot—reds and yellows and pinks and whites, some in full bloom, some still buds. "What am I going to do with these?"

Amazing, he thought. Two hundred dollars worth of flowers. Most women would be swooning or at least crooning. His beloved was complaining, apparently unimpressed and a little embarrassed.

"You're welcome," he said. His attempt to sound tough and arrogant ended up sounding, to his ears, sulky.

"Oh, hush, I love them and you know it." She leaned forward and hugged him, crushing the flowers between them. He didn't know which he liked better, the scent of the roses or the scent of her hair. He hugged her back, tightly. She looked out the window, suddenly thoughtful. "How are we getting to the restaurant?"

"Limo."

"Oh, ugh, do we have to? Can't we take the subway?"

He wasn't sure he had heard her correctly. "The subway?"

"Yeah, or walk. Is it walking distance? Do you have a car? Oh, forget it—I heard driving in Boston can be a pain."

"You don't want to take a limo?" He could feel his eyebrows arching up into his hairline. He knew her well enough by now to expect this sort of response, but still—it was a little hard to swallow. Who wouldn't jump at the chance to ride in a limousine? Jaded as he was, *he* still enjoyed it.

She thought he had taken offense. "Oh, don't get me wrong, Erik, limos are nice and all. It's just—you know, we're so lucky to have money, we can eat wherever we want and live wherever we want, and we don't have to work, not really, we just like to. And it doesn't seem fair to rub people's noses in it. Especially with all the homeless—I'd feel very self-conscious if we took a limo. It's kind of embarrassing, having money these days. Haven't you noticed?"

"You're amazing," he said before he thought.

"Nothing amazing about not wanting to be vulgar. No offense."

"Mmm. How about we take a cab?"

"A cab would be fine." A cab would be gross, he thought, but went to make the call.

"Let's wait outside until it gets here, okay? It's so nice and I haven't seen much of the neighborhood." She smoothed her skirt with one hand. "Is this okay for where we're going? Not too dressy? I wanted to dress up my first night in Boston."

"You look beautiful," he said, barely glancing at her as he dialed. He'd gotten more than an eyeful earlier when she'd made her entrance from the bedroom. She was wearing a black silk halter dress, black stockings and black pumps. Her only jewelry was a pair of gold hoop earrings. She had piled her glorious blonde hair on top of her head, letting a few errant strands and curls tumble down about her forehead and neck, and wore no makeup save for red lipstick. "You always look beautiful." He pretended to be engrossed in the wallpaper pattern. He didn't dare look at her for too long; she was exquisite and he might forget himself. And the really strange thing was, it wasn't just her stunning good looks that captivated him. He hung on her every word, her every gesture. He was like a smitten schoolboy around her— tongue-tied, embarrassed, never saying what he meant, and when he did say something it was usually cold or mean or both. It was aggravating as hell.

"Thank you. You look pretty good, too. Aren't we disgusting, two *nouveau riche* out on the town?" Stephanie privately thought that if Erik smiled a little more he would look even better. Not that there was anything wrong with his looks. They were both wearing black tonight —her in her little black dress and him in his black suit. The suit made his hair and eyes look darker than ever. She honestly felt he was the most handsome man she had ever seen, and wondered if people would think they made a nice couple.

"Come on, hon, the cab will be here in about ten minutes."

"Great!" And what was with all the endearments? Hon? Maybe he meant Hun, as in Attila. "I'm starved. I hope this place serves big meals." He helped her into her coat and prodded her out the door. "I don't like restaurants that serve little—oh, hello!"

The elevator attendant grinned and bowed her in with a flourish. Stephanie smiled. Erik scowled.

It was a long trip to the first floor. When they finally came to a stop, the attendant shouldered Erik back against the wall and gallantly presented Stephanie with his elbow. She took it and he helped her out of the elevator as if she were precious china. Bowing again, he disappeared into the elevator, leaving an impressed Stephanie and an irritated Erik.

"Good service here," she said.

"Remind me to move," Erik grumped, but would say no more, not even in response to her quizzical stare.

Their cab came, and he handed her inside, telling the cabbie where to take them, stealing a kiss when they were snuggled in the back. He could feel her lips against his, smiling, and he bent lower and kissed her neck. The smiling stopped then and he felt her stiffen against him.

"You're the most incredible woman I've ever met," he murmured. "Are you for real? You can't be real. This is an act, right? You're really a spoiled bitch, right?"

Stephanie was trying very hard to make out what he was saying, but it was terribly difficult with the light pressure of his lips against her throat. With just that one touch every coherent thought had fled her mind and she wondered if she would just slither out of his arms onto the floor, a little puddle of pleasure. His mouth against her throat...his breath as he murmured to her...it was driving her crazy. She wanted him to stop. She didn't want him to ever stop. She wanted to get out of this stupid confining dress and see if he could make her feel that way all over. She wanted to tell him she loved him. She wanted to tell him she didn't love him but she was attracted to him physically and would he please make love to her? She wanted to tell him that even though he was a jerk (some of the time...no, most of the time) she loved him anyway, even if he was ruined for love, even if he was sour on women forever. She wanted to tell him that no matter how it turned out with her father she didn't want him to ever leave her life.

She did none of these things. She heard a small sound escape her throat, a cross between a whimper and a groan. Erik chuckled, then nipped her lightly on her neck. She made a much louder sound, one much more like a groan than a whimper, and suddenly they were clinging to each other, making soft sounds of urgency in their throats, tongues exploring, hands gripping cloth. Stephanie's heart was pounding so loud she was sure the cabbie could—the cabbie!

She made a squeak of protest and tried to pull away. Erik dug in and pulled her back. She nipped lightly at his tongue, but his low growl was more one of pleasure than irritation.

She dug her index finger into his solar plexus, and his breath exploded into her mouth. He pulled back, coughing. "Okay, got it, no means no. What's wrong?"

Stephanie could feel the heat creeping up into her face, and gestured toward the cabbie, who was shouting in a foreign tongue at a car that had cut him off.

Erik looked. Saw nothing but a cabbie. Looked back at Stephanie, who was looking delightfully mussed and sexy as hell. His stomach throbbed. And dammit, his stomach was the only thing throbbing. God, he had to have her. Had to. Even if he had to marry her, he'd—

He'd—

Marry her?

Hmmm.

"I'm sorry about your foot," she was whispering. She leaned forward so the cabbie couldn't hear. Apparently, she wasn't aware of the inch-thick bullet proof glass between the front and back seats. "I got carried away—you're—you're an amazing kisser, did you know? Yes, you are. God, why am I telling you this? Like you're not arrogant enough. It's embarrassing how I—we—this isn't my idea of the ideal place and time, all right? In the back seat of a cab? Gross. Even if you are a great kisser."

Erik heard none of this. He was thinking harder than he ever had in his life. Marry her? Why not? She'd be his, then, not someone else's to pet and gloat over. He could show her everything, the world and all its people. They could take long trips together all over the world. She could have his children. Children? He'd never given ankle biters a second thought before, but the idea of a child that was part him, part Stephanie was deceptively attractive. And she could have his money. Hell, she had her own money, that was one of the great things about her. And best of all, she would be in his bed every night.

Every.

Night.

He'd avoided marriage to escape the connivers, of course, but also out of a desire to keep his options open. But for what? He'd never find an option better than Stephanie, not if he remained single for a hundred years.

"Erik? Hello? Are you listening to me?"

"Sure. I heard every word you said." They were less than a block from the restaurant, he pointed that fact out to Stephanie as he fished for his wallet. Marriage. Definitely something to think about. And never mind the feeling he was losing his mind. He saw the way the elevator man was looking at her. The thought of another man's hands on her body made him grit his teeth. She had to be his, had to. One way or the other.

"Erik, let me get it." She absently handed the cabbie a twenty and slammed the cab door shut while looking Kendall Square up and down.

He had chosen the Legal Sea Foods in Cambridge rather than the one in Boston because he liked the location better. A little less crowded, a little less hurried, Kendall Square was an attractive, romantic setting. A number of couples were strolling down the cobblestoned walks, window shopping.

"Come on, I can tell you're dying to get inside and commence stuffing your face," he teased, catching hold of her hand and pulling her into the restaurant. Stephanie was all eyes, looking at everything, staring at two men who left hand in hand, sniffing appreciatively at the delectable odors. In minutes, they were seated at a table by the window.

"Good spot," Stephanie said. The setting sun outside their window turned her pale skin to gold, turned her gold hair into red fire. Her eyes were very green. "I like to look out."

"I figured."

"Have whatever you like," she said, opening her menu.

"What?"

She looked over the top of the menu at him, amused and annoyed. Was there no room in his philosophy for a woman who didn't need a man to pay for everything? Good heavens, she and Sir probably had more money than he did. "I said, ave-hay atever-way oo-yay ike-lay. S'matter, Erik, you can't handle a woman paying for your meals?"

"It's rare, outside of business," he admitted, secretly annoyed. He had been hoping to use dinner as something of a lever. Dazzle her with good seafood, a little necking in the limo—err, cab—on the way back to the apartment...maybe he could coax her into...into...

Thinking of levers made him think of his original plan, the one he had come up with last night in her apartment. In the rush of events, he had completely forgotten it.

"Thank you. I will. Say, I was thinking of donating fifty thousand dollars for a soup kitchen in the Cities," he said suavely, leaning back in his chair and smiling at her.

"That's very kind. Suspiciously so. What's the catch? Do I have to go to bed with you or something? Mmmm, this lobster special looks yummy. Maybe the crab...I've never had raw oysters before. Are they any good?"

Ignoring the inner voice telling him this was a rotten idea, telling him to stop talking *now*, he leaned forward. "Think of all the people you'd be helping," he coaxed, catching hold of her hand. The menu fluttered to the floor. He rubbed his thumb across her knuckles and said in his lowest, most persuasive voice, the voice that talked CEO's into giving up their companies without a fight, "Fifty thousand dollars, a night of mind-boggling pleasure, and hundreds of people would benefit. Including you and me. Come on, Steph. Think about it."

She frowned at him. "You're serious, aren't you? I thought for a minute you were joking. Let's see...you and I have sex, and—"

"Make love," he interrupted.

"You and I do the wild thing, and in the morning you give me fifty thousand dollars to feed poor people with. My! I had no idea a prostitute could make so much money." She smiled, pulled her hand from his grasp and raised her water glass in a toast. "I think I'll decline your offer and give fifty thousand dollars of my money to the poor. And I won't tell them there are any strings attached." She took a sip, then with a sudden furious motion, threw the water in his face. "You're disgusting. How dare you proposition me? Do you think I'm one of your party girls, that you can nail me and then put me off with money? When are you going to get it through your thick, stupid skull that I'm not for sale? I'm me, Stephanie, and you're a jerk and I can't *believe* I'm here having dinner with you." Her tirade ended with a furious whisper and she shot up from her seat. A waiter hurried over.

"Sir, madam, is there something I can—"

"Yes," Erik said, also standing up, feeling like the world's biggest ass. Water trickled down his neck. He wiped more out of his eyes. Coughed a little. "You can get me a towel. I've behaved disgracefully to the lady and she let me have it."

The waiter looked from one to the other. Stephanie didn't notice, she was too busy glaring at Erik. What a low down, sneaky creep he was! And what did that make her, for wanting him?

"Please don't leave, Steph. You're right, I was a jerk." Aarrgh! He hated apologizing. Especially when he was wrong. "I honestly didn't think about it in terms of prostitution. I didn't. I know you're not like the others. With the others, dinner and dancing would have done it. I wanted to think of something really big to give you if you'd sleep with me. I tried to play on your good nature and I screwed up. It's just...I want you so badly, I'm not thinking straight. Please forgive me. Stay and have dinner. Please?"

Stephanie could feel herself thawing. Just a little, though. She still thought he was a creep. But he wanted her. He said so, in front of the waiter and everyone else in the restaurant. And she wanted him. Did that make her bad? Or just stupid?

She sat. Still frowning, she picked up her menu and started looking at it again. The waiter vanished.

"Steph. I know you're still mad. C'mon, have mercy." He was

using that voice again, the one that she felt rather than heard. Like velvet, it was soothing, soft, caressing. She could feel the goosebumps raising along her arms. "How can I make it up to you? In a way that doesn't include you taking your clothes off?"

She smiled behind the menu, then frowned again and looked at him. "I hate it when you treat me like a brainless whore."

He winced. Water trickled into his collar and dripped onto his shirt and he shivered. She felt a smile plucking at her lips and fought it.

"You're right. You're so right. I'm really, really, really sorry. Ever since I've met you I've been saying all the wrong things and doing—"

"Actually, you've been acting like yourself, but what works with everyone else isn't working with me, so you come off looking like an ass. And you never answered my question."

Question? What question? He must have looked blank, because she added, "Are raw oysters any good?"

"They're delicious. I think you'll like them a lot." Relieved she was giving him a way out, he slicked his wet hair back and sighed a little. "Please let me pick up the dinner tab. To make it up to you. So I don't feel like a total idiot."

She was trying very, very hard to hold on to her anger. It wasn't working at all. "Erik, I'll tell you something. No matter how horrible and creepy you act, it's hard for me to stay mad at you. And that's the truth."

"Well, thank God for that," he muttered, and smiled at her. "It's probably the only thing that keeps saving me."

"Your towel, sir." The waiter handed Erik a fluffy white towel as if water being thrown at dinner guests was an everyday occurrence. Perhaps in Boston, it was. "Are you ready to order?"

"Oh, yes! I'm starving. Erik, you ready? Good. I'll have a frozen mudslide for starters, and the raw oysters for an appetizer, and the lobster, and then I'll probably want dessert so can you come back?"

"Certainly, madam. May I pour you more water? You seem to be out. And for the gentleman?"

"The same." Damned if he wasn't going to keep up with her.

"Excellent. Oh, thank you, sir," as Erik handed him back the towel. His hair stood up in wet, unruly spikes. He shivered a little. "Perhaps a hot toddy, instead?"

"No. Frozen mudslide. And keep 'em coming."

"Trying to get me drunk?"

"No, trying to get me drunk. Then I won't be responsible for my actions," he said, still angry at himself for how he'd treated her.

"Oh, Erik," Stephanie said. "Such a terrible time you've had since you startled me into banging my head under the desk."

"I'm one big bruise, top to bottom."

"Poor thing."

"You're out to get me."

"Poor baby."

And then it really was okay, he could feel it. She was grinning at him in that go-to-hell-if-you-can't-take-a-joke way and something inside him loosened.

The drinks and appetizers came. Stephanie looked doubtfully at the ring of oyster shells on her plate. Erik scooted his chair over to help. "It's really easy, sweetie. Just take the little fork—yes, that one, like that—and loosen the oyster right here, and just pick up the shell—yes, with your fingers, that's all right, and just tilt and slurp it down. Don't chew. Just swallow."

"Really? That's how you're supposed to eat these things?" She looked doubtful, but did as he instructed. Lifting the shell to her mouth, she tilted and sucked it down. It slid down her throat like pudding, and tasted about a hundred times better. "Oh, wow, that's good!" she exclaimed, scooping up another one and sending it the way of the first. "Yum! Mmmm. Here, you have one." She fed him an oyster, and then he fed her one. Maybe it was the texture of the food, or the fact that his fingers were near her mouth, but she began to feel very warm. And hadn't she read somewhere that raw oysters were an aphrodisiac?

On impulse, she kissed him. He put a hand on the back of her neck and kissed her back, slowly, lingeringly. She trembled a little as fire uncoiled in her middle. "Here, have another one," she said unsteadily, pulling back and feeding him. His eyes never left hers. She noticed her hands were shaking and folded them in her lap. "Good stuff."

"You feel it, too. I was wondering if it was just my imagination. Does it scare you?" he asked quietly.

"Does what scare me?" she asked, studying her hands as if she had never seen them before.

"Us. What happens when we touch. Or even when we don't. Because I'll tell you the truth, my dear. It scares the hell out of me."

Stephanie's eyes widened. Erik? Scared? "Why? Me, too, by the way, but I'll bet for a different reason."

"Why? What, you don't know?" Erik laughed and ran a hand through his hair, trying unsuccessfully to smooth it back. "Because I've never met anyone like you, and I've certainly never felt this way about—well, I did, once, but it wasn't like this. And I'll be frank, Stephanie, I don't much care for feeling like a bull in rut whenever I'm around you. It's embarrassing and frustrating. I'm not used to being out of control."

Stephanie could feel her face grow warm. He was being quite frank with her, and she found it unsettling. And did she really make him feel like a bull in rut? Gross.

"I've embarrassed you. I'm sorry. I thought it would be nice to be straight with you for a change."

"And I appreciate it," she said hastily. "I'll try and return the favor. Ever since I met you, I haven't been able to figure you out. Really! First you're mean to me, then you're a sweetheart, then you're mean, then you're nice again—it's driving me crazy! And there are times when I think you're going to warm up a little and then you're an absolute jerk—worse than ever. Like after dinner last night. And in the cab today. What's the matter with me, that makes you act like such a weirdo?"

"Nothing! Nothing. It's me. My problem is, I can't figure out what to do with you."

"What, like I'm a stray dog or something?" She tried to smile. It felt wrong on her face, fake. She quit trying.

"No." He started to say something else, stopped, tried to start again, and then the waiter came with their salads. Stephanie could have screamed.

After five minutes of silence, broken only by the clink of cutlery as they picked at their salads, Stephanie had had enough.

"Can I ask you something, and know you'll tell the truth?"

He looked up, surprised. "Sure."

"I mean it," she said. What she was about to address had been nagging at her all day—indeed, since last night. "You lie all the time...at least to me, but I need the truth now."

His eyes narrowed when she called him a liar, but he could hardly deny it, so he shrugged and smiled instead, and promised to tell the truth, even raising a hand in the Boy Scout salute.

"What's wrong with my father?"

Apparently that wasn't the question he had been expecting, because he stared at her in the strangest way. "What did you say?" he managed at last.

"I said, what's wrong with my father? I mean, I know he left me when I was a baby because he was upset Mama died, but you've been super-nice to me all damn day—since last night, actually—and I know it's because you're trying to cushion a blow I've no idea is heading my way. So be straight with me, please, Erik, and tell me what's wrong."

"I've met a lot of women in the last few years—"

"Yeah, I know."

"—but you've got to be the sharpest." He shook his head ruefully. "Was I that obvious?"

"Just answer the question, all right? I'm tired of being handled like a balloon about to pop," she snapped.

"All right, all right, don't pitch your salad at me. Nothing's really wrong with your father...he's a smart man. Brilliant, actually. He's made a lot of money and he took good care of my mother and me."

"But."

He considered how to tell her that her father was the meanest son of a bitch to walk the planet. He opted for tact. "I think when your mother died, part of him—maybe most of him—went with her. He's not the nicest guy in the world. He's pretty ruthless in business."

"But so are you," Stephanie interjected. "Sir let me read up on you and your company, when I still thought I was supposed to be your agent. And remember, *Business Week* did that not-so-flattering article about you and Chambers and Associates. 'The most mercenary consulting firm operating in America' was how they put it, I believe."

He grinned. "Yeah. That was a great story. Brought in lots of business. And you've got a good point."

"So stop pussy-footing around, you big chicken, and be straight with me for once."

Erik shrugged. "I hate him. Straight enough for you? I think he's an immoral bastard. He doesn't care about anyone but himself. He treats my mother like garbage—although to be fair she treats him pretty badly, too—and he's never had a thing to do with me. He cheats on my mother, she cheats on him. They're only married on paper. I can't forgive her for marrying him."

Stephanie put her chin in her hand and thought about this. It wasn't much of a surprise—Sir hadn't painted a pretty picture when he described Brian's actions after her birth.

"I think you're being too hard on your mother," she said at last. "She did what she had to do, to keep the two of you together."

Erik barked laughter. The sound was loud and harsh in the restaurant. Heads turned toward them, not for the first time. "My mother has an MBA from Harvard—just like your father. She was making plenty when she married my dad, but when he died she despaired at the idea of actually having to work for a living. Her problem is, she's always wanted to be rich and idle. Living the life of a society wife. Afternoon luncheons, charity work with the other hens, that sort of thing. When she got a look at your father's bankbook she jumped for him. And the rest, as they say, is history."

"I'm sorry," Stephanie said quietly.

"You and me both, blondie," Erik said. He downed the rest of his drink in three gulps.

"I've got my work cut out for me, don't I?"

"What work? You're going to walk into his office, tell him who you are, and then you and I are getting the hell out."

"We'll see," she said with an enigmatic smile.

They finished their meal with no further outbursts or arguments. Stephanie declared it one of the finest she'd ever had and ordered two desserts—the chocolate amaretto mousse and the strawberry cheesecake—when she couldn't decide between the two. Erik, on the other hand, had trouble finishing his meal and had to decline dessert.

"I've never seen someone eat so much," he said with an expression close to wonder. "It's amazing. I'm having trouble with my coffee, for God's sake. Will you slow down? No one's going to take it away from you."

"It's so good, I can't help it," Stephanie said with her mouth full. "Are you going to finish your brussels sprouts?"

"We'll have to roll you away from the table," he muttered, but still pushed his plate toward her.

"Oh, come on! I haven't had that much. Do you think we could get some ice cream on the way home?"

Erik groaned and covered his eyes.

"Tip the waiter big," Stephanie said. "He put up with our garbage all night."

"I was tipping waiters when you were yet unborn," Erik sneered, fishing out his MasterCard.

"What, when you were four? I don't think so."

She fell asleep in the cab, her head on his shoulder, her body snuggled against his. He slipped an arm around her and thought about the evening. Despite his blunder with the poor house offering, and Stephanie hearing not-so-nice things about her father, the evening had gone reasonably well. They hadn't thrown their dinners at each other, at any rate.

He hoped he could persuade her to stay with him a few more days after her father blew her out of the water, though she would probably want to put as many miles as she could between her and Boston after she met the gentleman.

The thing about Brian Dares that made him a genius at business was just this: he could shut things (companies, people, lawsuits, contracts) out of his mind with no trouble. Could make himself not think about them at all. This had stood him in good stead during many a corporate takeover, and was probably the only reason the man could sleep at night. So when Stephanie announced herself, he would throw her out and then dismiss her from his mind, forever. His immediate concern would be to get her out of his sight as quickly as possible, then he would make himself forget her. Unless Stephanie showed up every day until the man died, Brian would win.

Unless...

The glimmerings of an idea began to form in Erik's mind, an idea that would prevent Brian from shutting his daughter out, an idea that would solve his and Stephanie's current problems very neatly.

It was a frightening prospect, this plan, and he wondered if he would have the courage to go through with it. It would mean baring his heart to a woman...again. It would mean setting himself up for a long, long fall...again.

The alternative, however, was just as unthinkable.

Chapter 12

STEPHANIE LAY in bed, arms crossed behind her head, looking up at the ceiling. It was very late, her stomach was full, and under these circumstances she normally dropped off in seconds. Tonight, however, sleep was unobtainable. She had a lot to think about.

Meeting her father was in the back of her mind, but Erik was foremost in her thoughts tonight. He'd been strangely preoccupied since they got back to his apartment, and she wondered what he was thinking. Perhaps he was worrying about tomorrow, as she was.

Her bed seemed too big and suddenly she was so lonely and afraid she thought her heart would break. What was she doing in this strange city, far away from Sir, who was more of a father than this Brian had ever been? She didn't belong here. She didn't want to be here. Her land was the Midwest, with miles of fields and flatlands. Not this strange, fuming city by the sea, where no one knew her or cared if she lived or died.

She got up. She was wearing a green flannel nightshirt, cut just below her knees. It was comfortable and made her feel good. She hoped it wouldn't look too provocative to Erik. She didn't want him to get the wrong idea.

Then she thought of making love with him and felt her whole body blush. She wanted him, there was no question, but she couldn't give herself to a man who didn't know what he wanted, a man who couldn't decide if he cared for her or couldn't stand the sight of her. And her conscience wouldn't let her surrender to her body's needs.

Dammit, she thought, creeping out into the hallway. Why couldn't I be loose and get it over with? I'm twenty-three, for heaven's sake. Nothing to be afraid of.

But she was afraid, there was no denying that. Not so much afraid of Erik as afraid of what happened between them whenever their gazes locked, whenever they chanced to touch.

Erik's door was open. She paused before entering, then braced herself and walked in.

He was awake, waiting for her. Without a word, he held the covers back so she could climb in.

"I was hoping you'd come," he said. His voice was rough in the dark.

She snuggled against his chest, so comfortable she felt like purring. "I almost didn't. I was afraid you'd take liberties."

"You're right. How can I resist you in the big green tablecloth you're wearing?"

She poked him in the stomach, then did it again when he laughed at her. He caught her hands and held them, tightly. "You oaf!" she said with mock anger, wriggling to get free without hurting him (too much). "It's a nightshirt. I can't help it if it's a little big on me."

"A little? You were lost in the thing."

"It's super comfortable."

"And super silly looking."

"And I was afraid you'd find me too seductive."

"I do," he said seriously. "I find you maddeningly seductive. You could wear a potato sack and I'd still think you were irresistible." He let go of her arms long enough for her to slip them behind his neck, and then kissed her deeply. The feel of her warm body next to his was driving him mad. He wanted nothing more than to hold her and make love to her all night, until they were both spent. With a groan, he pulled back and lay down beside her. "Enough of that, before I rape you."

"Good luck," Stephanie said smugly, if a little breathlessly. "Try anything and I'll have to break something."

He mock-growled, grabbed her hand, and bit her lightly on the wrist. She clenched a fist and bopped him on the nose. Their play made Erik wonder if he'd ever goofed around in bed with a woman. Not sexual playing—just having fun and horsing around, as he and Stephanie were. He realized he hadn't wanted to before this because there had never been a woman he could have fun with.

"I was engaged once," he said, pretending this wasn't difficult for him.

"I figured." She turned on her side and curled up against him. "What was her name?"

"Margaret. Margaret Bitchwoman Gottlieb." He laughed ruefully at how petulant he sounded. "At least that's what I started calling her, after."

"Was she pretty?"

"Yes. I guess. Not as pretty as you. She was a redhead. Little thing. Came up to my shoulder—barely. Very ambitious." Very hot in bed, he remembered, but decided not to bring it up. "She wanted to be a doctor."

The rage he felt for so long whenever he thought of Margaret

(Bitchwoman) Gottlieb was curiously absent. What he felt most was regret. Regret that they had parted badly. Regret that he had let this bother him for so long. They had been young and the young are ruthless.

"Is she a doctor now?"

"She better be. She took the money and ran."

"What money?"

He was silent for a long time. Stephanie wondered if she had pushed too hard. She was dying to hear this story, which would probably explain away much of Erik's animosity toward women. She was glad he trusted her enough to tell her.

"My mother...disapproved of Margaret. Remember I told you my mother wanted to be a society wife? She made herself believe she was from old money. Gave herself airs. And she got the idea into her head Margaret wasn't good enough for me. She had visions of me marrying a princess of the realm or something. Anyway, she went to see Margaret about a week after we announced our engagement. I think she realized how badly Margaret wanted to get her medical degree. She had years of school ahead of her and I wasn't very well established yet. Hell, I was still in school myself, I wasn't established at all. So my mother offered my bride-to-be five hundred thousand dollars to stay away from me. Ample money to pursue her degree and live well, besides. And when she got out of school, a little nest egg to get her started. All in all, a nice package. So what do you think my bride-to-be did?"

"Told you mother to drop dead?" Stephanie asked. Obviously not, she told herself. After all, Erik isn't married, is he?

"Nope. Said, thank you very much, where do I sign, goodbye, Erik, it's been fun." He laughed. The pain was clear in his voice. Not the pain of unrequited love, because he doubted he'd been truly in love with Margaret at all. Oh, he'd been in lust with her, all right. She'd had a tight little body that he couldn't get enough of. But the pain he felt, and had felt from the day she left, was the pain of betrayal. "In the movies the heroine throws the offer back in the antagonist's face and the couple lives happily ever after. In real life, almost no one can resist the temptation of money."

"If she'd truly loved you, she wouldn't have left," Stephanie said, burning. Margaret Bitchwoman Gottlieb had better hope she never ran into Stephanie Veronica Dares, by God.

"She didn't truly love me," he replied dryly. "I was furious with my mother, but madder at Margaret. After all, my mother didn't make her take the money. Just dangled it in front of her like a..."

"Plump, juicy worm," Stephanie finished. "The ugly little brook trout. So that's who I have to thank for you being such a creep. But why the big confession?"

Erik shrugged. "Thought you deserved an explanation for my boorish personality. There it is."

"I'm glad you didn't marry her, too," Stephanie said. "Otherwise, I'd be fooling around with a married man. Unless you divorced her in the first two years, which sounds likely."

"Oh, Steph, you're so wise," Erik said with mock awe. "How did I ever get along without your sage advice? How did I—ouch!"

"You had that coming."

"And you have this coming," he said, kissing her gently, and then more urgently, and then plundering her mouth with the air of a starving man denied nourishment too long. Her mouth was so sweet, he could kiss her for hours and never grow tired of her taste, her feel.

Stephanie felt herself pressed back into the pillows, felt Erik's mouth moving on hers, and parted her lips to mate her tongue with his. She could feel his body, long and lean and hard, pressing against hers, and a wave of desire swept over her that was stunning in its size and power. Had she ever felt this way in her life? Had any woman?

She could feel his hands on her body, on her breasts. Her nipples strained through the fabric and when he moved his hands restlessly across them, they hardened to impudent peaks. Stephanie groaned helplessly.

Erik began to unbutton her pajamas with the care of a man who isn't sure his hands will do as he bids. They were shaking so, the small buttons were giving him considerable trouble. Finally he muttered an oath and, with a rending tear the fabric parted, baring her breasts. She gasped at the sound. *Her favorite tablecloth*, he thought with grim amusement. *I'll have to buy her another one tomorrow.* She gasped again as he lowered his mouth to a pink peak. He sucked gently, then turned his attention to the whole breast, licking and sucking and kissing the creamy skin, her throaty whimpers getting him as hot as caressing her flesh was. God, she was so smooth and warm and alive beneath his hands, her breath coming in shorter and shorter pants, wriggling beneath him as she sought to give him better access.

When his mouth left her nipple she thought she would die. But he lingered over her breasts, caressing and kissing and licking and sucking until she thought she would die or go crazy or both. Her hands fisted in his hair. She could feel a slow, delicious warmth uncoiling in her loins and, responding to a primitive urge fed by her body's lust, she spread her legs, quite unconsciously. He responded by settling between them and rolling over until she was on top. He caught one nipple in his mouth as she arched over him, her skin marbling into gooseflesh. Her nightshirt gaped open, revealing her lovely body to him.

Erik felt the world spin away from him as he pressed his face between her breasts. His breath came in harsh pants as he fought to control the urge to fling her on her back and surge into her with one hard thrust. Had he ever been so overcome, so close to losing control? Hadn't sex always been, to him, an exercise in pleasure only? Easily obtained and completely forgettable? Not this—this sharing?

"God, you are so amazing! What are you doing to me?" Their lips met again, and while their tongues danced he let his hands roam all over her lovely length, an urge he had had since he first laid eyes on her. She was exquisite. There was no other word for how she looked and felt to him. Smooth long limbs, flat stomach, saucily curved buttocks, full and lovely breasts.

His hands were...everywhere. She gloried in his hands on her body, making her feel cherished, making her his lover. His mouth was against her throat, his hands were on her breasts. "I like that," she managed. "I—" Words failed her as a shudder racked her frame. He was amazing! He knew her body better than she did.

"Oh, me too, me too," he groaned, rolling her on her back. "You'll like this better." He reached down, past her flat stomach and down the slope of her pubis, his fingers caressing the downy fluff that shielded her most intimate spot from him. Her legs were spread invitingly, her tongue darting in his ear, and his fingers slid down and found her satiny dampness. "I need you so much, sweetheart," he rasped. "I've been dreaming about this since I met you."

She shoved against his chest, hard. At the touch of his fingers between her thighs, reason surged back.

"Don't—don't do that!" she gasped, squirming away from him. Passion was being replaced by fear and embarrassment. Handsome rogue though he was, he looked quite sinister to her just then and she wondered if she had a real fight on her hands. "Please, Erik, we have to stop." He was so astonished he let her go with no resistance and she surged from the bed, pulling the remnants of her nightshirt around her and running for her room.

She slammed the door and stood there, panting. Her body throbbed with need. Her face was red with shame. How could she face Erik in the morning? How could she ever face him again? She wanted to die.

A fist hammered against the door. "Stephanie? Are you all right? Stephanie?" He sounded frantic, worried, and as out of breath as she was. Not mad, though. That was something. "Did I hurt you, sweetheart? Please let me in."

"I'm okay," she said in a cracked voice. She opened the door, remembering too late her nightshirt no longer offered modest covering. She pulled it about her as he caught her up in his arms, running his hands over her limbs. Not with passion, but with care, searching for an injury.

"Are you all right? What's the matter?" His concern made her want to weep. He was so thoughtful, worried about her and not his own pressing need. She loved him.

To her shame and his dismay, she started to cry.

"We can't. You and I. I'm sorry. And I'm afraid," she sobbed.

"Oh, honey, I had protection, I wasn't going to let you get preg--"

"I'm a virgin," she gulped, weeping afresh as she saw the shock on his face. "Please. We can't."

He seemed utterly at a loss for a moment. She didn't know what he was thinking. It was probably just as well.

Then he smiled and a terrible weight lifted from her heart. "A virgin! God almighty, I should have guessed. You poor thing, you must have been terrified." He hugged her and kissed her on the mouth, lovingly, without heat, then held her by the shoulders and looked at her with tenderness. "Did I scare you, sweetheart?"

"Only at the end," she said, calming at how well he was taking the news. "I wasn't scared of you, exactly, I was scared of me. Of how you made me feel. I had to stop us or it would have been too late."

"It sure would have," he said ruefully. A virgin! He still couldn't believe it. Of all the things he had been afraid she would say, that had to be the one he least expected. The primitive part of him was thrilled that she was untouched. The not-so-primitive part of him was, too. "I've never been with a virgin." He paused, frowned. "Not even when I was one."

"Let's leave your loose past out of this," she said, disgruntled. She shoved him away and covered her face with her hands. "I'm so embarrassed. You must think I'm a...slut or something, for letting you do that to me."

"Yes. Stephanie Dares, Virgin Whore," he said, then laughed as she glared at him. He hugged her fiercely. "I'm so relieved, I thought you were going to say I hurt you or you were married or something."

He looked at her. "I wish you had told me. I would have gone a lot slower if I had known."

"I didn't want you to know."

"Why not?"

"I was afraid you'd laugh at me."

"Laugh at you? What for?"

"Because." She faltered a bit, searching for a way to put her shame into words. "I know I must seem very old-fashioned to you, with your experience, but I just can't bring myself to make love unless—unless it's real. And I was afraid to tell you because you've been so—well, it seems to me that there's some physical attraction here." She could feel herself getting red. Erik, bless him, didn't say a word, just let her finish. She wrenched the rest of the words out. "And I was afraid if you knew I was a virgin and didn't want a one-night stand, you wouldn't like me anymore. And I need you to like me. I need you to like me a lot." Feeling wretched, she burst into tears. She had made a mess of things, as usual. He would think her a silly twit—a silly virginal twit—and make her go away. She would have to face her father by herself. She would have to face the rest of her life by herself.

"Stephanie, this isn't worth crying about. And I like you fine. I think it's great that you're still a virgin." He tenderly wiped away her tears with the tips of his fingers. "Not many people have the courage to stand by what they believe in, but you do it and you don't care what people think about it. I think that's terrific." He cupped her chin and kissed her on the lips. "I think you're terrific."

"Really?" she squeaked, unable to believe her good fortune. He understood! By some miracle.

"Really. And I only have one question and then we can go back to bed."

"What?"

"Why did you let us get so far, if you didn't want to make love? If you're saving yourself for when it's real."

"I—" She closed her mouth with a snap. Thought carefully before she answered. Then gave him as much truth as she dared. "I guess I just got carried away." She wouldn't tell him how she felt. Not until she had a better idea what his feelings were. She had slipped once, and in his fright, he had been cruel. She wouldn't let him do it again.

"Really? That's the only reason?"

"Uh-huh," she said, and she wouldn't look at him.

"Fair enough," he said, not believing that was all by a long shot. She wasn't going to let him in. Erik wasn't really surprised. He had given her no reason to trust him with her feelings. In fact, as horribly as he had treated her, he was lucky she was here at all.

Coward that he was, though, he couldn't make it easier between them by telling the truth—that he loved her dearly, had loved her since he first laid eyes on her, and wanted to marry her and raise children with her and grow old with her.

He knew she liked him a lot, else she wouldn't have let them go so far a few minutes ago. He would wait until she wasn't afraid, until she told him she loved him, and then he would tell her the same.

Happy for the first time in three days, he led her back to his bed, swore up and down to her that he would keep his hands to himself, and tucked them both under the covers. She curled up against his side like a sleepy kitten and was asleep in minutes.

He watched her for an hour, occasionally smoothing her hair or running his fingers through the golden strands, content just to look at her, and be near her, and love her. Much later, he went to sleep himself.

In the wee hours of the morning, she woke up, trembling and afraid from a nightmare in which her father screamed that this was the wretched girl who had killed his wife.

Erik was there, soothing her as best he could, telling her that her father would love her as he loved her, whispering that she was perfect and her father would know this, as he knew it. Stephanie would remember none of this in the morning, but Erik never forgot how she fell asleep clinging to him, not relaxing her grip even when slumber claimed her.

Chapter 13

SHE SPENT THE morning in the bathroom, victim of a nervous stomach. Erik shouted through the bathroom door that they could put off the meeting until tomorrow. Stephanie shouted back that she'd be damned if she was going through this two days in a row and emerged an hour later, pale and composed. She had dressed with special care, and nervously asked Erik how she looked.

"You look great. Really terrific," he said. And despite her too-pale face, she really did look beautiful. The suit was dark red, making her skin and hair look even lighter. The skirt was short, showing off long legs, and the jacket was buttoned over a white blouse. She looked every inch the cool professional.

She downed the coffee he held out to her in three gulps. Luckily, it had had ample time to cool. "Let's go before I change my mind."

Brian Chambers' office was in the financial district. Traffic was light and they were there by noon. Stephanie checked her watch as she climbed from the limo and said, somewhat hopefully, "Won't he be out to lunch?"

"If he is, we'll wait. Probably won't be out, though. He's a big fan of brown-bagging it." Erik knew his stepfather never went out to lunch unless it would profit him somehow. "Smile, Steph. You look great and everyone's looking at you. Let's go up." He took her by the arm and steered her toward the entrance. She was still too pale, but at least she was moving under her own power. *Jeez, you'd think this was my idea,* he thought, propelling her through the door. *Is this the same woman who dared Sir and me to stop her from going to Boston yesterday morning? She looks like she's going to faint. Or throw up. Or both.*

They took the elevator to the fourth floor. On the way up, Stephanie tried to control the butterflies-or were they bald eagles?-carooming around in her stomach. *Sure you're nervous,* she told herself. *It's perfectly natural to be nervous. You want to make a good impression on the man who abandoned you as an infant. And you will. You will. Just think positive.*

Look at Erik. He looks great, not nervous at all. He's so beautiful. It's a wonder he's not vain. There—he smiled at me. He's full of optimism. He's been so helpful and kind, I just know it'll work out. It has to. And is he thinking about last night as much as I am? It was wonderful until I made him stop. Too bad in a way, it certainly felt—

"Our stop, Steph," Erik said. The elevator door stood open and he stood back to let her pass. For some reason her face was red. Stress, probably. Or was she thinking about last night? Lord knew he certainly couldn't get last night out of his mind. "Straight ahead."

She saw the door past the receptionist. Saw the stenciled window: BRIAN CHAMBERS, PRESIDENT AND CEO. Gulped. Moved back to let Erik pass.

"Hi, Karen. Is Brian in?"

Karen, the receptionist, tried not to gape and failed. Stephanie assumed it was rare for the stepson to make an appearance in the Hated Office. "Yes, Bri—yes, sir, he's in with your mother. They're planning his birthday party."

"Your mother's here, too?" Stephanie asked faintly. This was getting better and better.

"You know what they say about swimming," Erik said cheerfully, yanking open the door to his stepfather's domain. "Jump in and get it over with. None of this inch by inch garbage."

She managed a smile and strode through the door.

The first person she noticed was Erik's mother. What was her name? Had Erik told her? The woman was petite and dark-haired, probably in her late fifties. She might have been pretty if she let herself age with grace, but she was dressed and made-up like someone twenty years younger and the effect was startling and a little sad. Her dark hair was cut short, framing her face. Her eyebrows were plucked into two thin lines, her nose was a blade, her lips thin and, when she spotted Stephanie, pressed tightly together.

She spoke. Her voice was cultured, low, controlled. Much like Erik's. "You can have him when I'm through, honey. Are you the mistress *du jour*?"

Erik was right behind her, shutting the door. "Hardly. She's with me, mother."

Her father looked up from his work and, for a moment, Stephanie thought the man was going to have a heart attack. His face, which was dark and leathery from years outdoors, lost all color. His eyes, a brilliant, piercing green, widened until it seemed they must fall out of his head.

My God, Stephanie thought, drinking him in. *Do my eyes look like that to people? So hard and sharp?*

He started to rise, changed his mind, sank back in his chair, never taking his eyes off Stephanie.

His wife missed none of this, and her voice was quite a lot sharper when she snapped, "Brian! What's the matter with you? Have you and Erik fixated on the same woman? Who is she? You look like death."

Stephanie took advantage of the man's total surprise and jumped. "I'm so sorry to barge in on you like this, Mr. Chambers, but I thought it was time you and I met. We were never properly introduced." She stepped forward, past the woman. Her father stared and stared. His mouth was hanging open. He was still pale. "My name is Stephanie Veronica Dares. I believe you knew my mother."

"Veronica," he whispered.

"Veronica?" his wife shrilled. "Veronica Dares? You mean this is your *daughter*?"

"That's right. Might I have the pleasure of your name, ma'am?"

"Marcy," the woman said, now staring at Stephanie with an expression of shock and amazement. An expression identical to her husband's. Behind her, Erik laughed and smothered it in his fist. "I mean—Marceline Chambers."

Behind the desk, Brian Chambers had apparently regained his wits. He jumped to his feet and Stephanie had time to notice he was tall, extremely tall, almost six five, and extremely thin. So that's where I get it from, she thought distantly.

"Out!" Brian roared. His arm shot out and he swept his desk clean of the clutter of papers. "Out! Get out of my office, you hateful, murdering bitch!" He looked around wildly, probably for something to throw. Erik lunged forward, leaning across the massive desk and grabbing his stepfather by the lapels. He yanked the man forward.

"Don't talk to her like that, you bastard," he hissed, eyeball to eyeball with the bane of his existence. He was so furious he could hardly see. The man had reacted exactly as Erik had predicted, but for once, being right was little comfort. "You just shut your mouth right now, do you understand me? Just shut. The hell. Up."

Stephanie noticed Erik was shorter than her father, but broader. The part of her that wasn't horrified was noticing everything, it seemed. Her father was lean and hard and terribly tall. He looked like his body had burned up everything superfluous in his personality and left slate behind. Erik, in comparison, looked like the angel Gabriel, so marked was the contrast. *Did I really think Erik was hard when I first met him? Good God, I didn't know what hard was...*

Brian tried to free himself, with difficulty, from his stepson's grasp. Erik had calmed down a bit and let go, but not without giving the man a helpful shove backward. He backed away from the desk and took Stephanie's arm.

He still looked angry enough to tear the man's heart out, but his voice was calm and controlled when he said, "I might have known you'd react like this. In fact, I did know. I tried to warn her what an incredible bastard you are, but she wanted to meet you anyway. That's what a great person she is. Not that you know, or care." He turned to Stephanie. She noticed his scar had turned white and there was a tic working at the corner of his mouth. "Seen enough, hon?"

"Oh, yes." She manufactured a smile and flashed it at her father. The man, perhaps seeing much of his wife in that smile, flinched backward and nearly fell. "I'm glad we finally got the chance to meet. I'll be back when you've had time to consider your good fortune." She nodded at Erik's mother. "Good day, ma'am. Erik, shall we—?"

"We shall," he said gallantly, picking up on her intent. If she wanted to go down smiling, so be it. He held the door open for her and she swept through, shoulders back, head high, long legs carrying her out the door and out of her father's line of sight.

Erik followed her out, pausing to look back and chide, "I think you could have handled that better, Brian, don't you?"

The man cursed and hurled a glass ashtray—the only thing left on his desk—at his stepson. It came nowhere close, missing Erik by a good three feet and shattering the glass window beside him. BRIAN CHAMBERS, PRESIDENT AND CEO broke into a thousand pieces and littered the carpet.

"Temper, temper, Bri," Erik tsked and closed the door.

In the reception area, Stephanie was giving Erik's number to the stunned receptionist, who was looking at the broken glass with drugged horror. "He can reach me here if he'd like," Stephanie was saying. "I assume he's got the number but I'm taking no chances. You never can tell with this family. You will give it to him, won't you?"

"Yes, ma'am," the receptionist whispered, taking the card with trembling fingers.

"Thank you. If you will permit me, I must say that you look unwell. Perhaps you should take some time off. Things around here are likely to be..." She looked at the broken glass and smiled wryly. "...explosive."

"Yes, ma'am."

"Goodbye."

"Goodbye, ma'am."

From behind them, a roar. "Out!"

"I'm going, I'm going," Stephanie muttered. That was the last thing she said for hours.

Chapter 14

THEY WERE sitting in the sand on Sandwich Beach. It was another beautiful autumn day and there were quite a few other people walking or sitting on the beach, but none came near the two of them. It was as if passers-by sensed the misery Stephanie was giving off in waves.

He had driven her to the beach after swinging by his apartment to change. Coming back down to the parking lot, Stephanie had climbed into his car without asking where they were going. She fell asleep almost immediately, so Erik had much of the drive to Cape Cod to think about his plan. He had decided last night to do it, but the presentation of his idea needed refinement. He worked it out on the way to the beach.

Stephanie still hadn't said anything, but she'd brightened when she saw the beach and walked up to the water's edge without hesitation. She stood looking out at the sea for a long time, then sank down in the sand and started to build a sand castle. It wasn't going to be much of one—not with just her bare hands—but she seemed restless, seemed to need something to do. Erik joined her, and they worked silently for some minutes.

Finally, she spoke. "That didn't go as well as I thought." Her voice was low, calm. She concentrated on building the moat for their castle and didn't look up.

"I know." Had he ever felt such pain for someone? Even for himself? He knew he had not. "I'm sorry."

"Nothing to be sorry about. You told me what he was like." She laughed a little. The sound was like breaking glass, not his darling's throaty chuckle. "I guess I thought I was so irresistible he'd sweep me up in his arms and be my father."

"You are irresistible. Look how you've got me trying to jump your delectable bones all the time. Give him time. He'll come around. If I thought anyone could wake that man up I'd put my money on you. God's truth."

"Thank you. I will try. May I stay with you for a few more days?"

"Of course. I was going to ask you to stay if you hadn't asked first. But you have to sleep in my bed."

"You have to behave."

"I promise. I'll stop when you want. In fact, I won't start unless you want. In fact, let's pretend we're monks."

She looked up and he was alarmed to see tears shimmering in those great green eyes. He had tried to cheer her up as best he could but he wasn't used to treating people with gentle affection and had obviously bungled it. "Oh, please don't, sweetheart," he groaned. "It's killing me to see you so upset. And he's not worth your tears."

"He can't stand the sight of me," she said, still calm, but two tears spilled from those eyes and down her face. "Did you see his face? I thought he was going to drop dead on the spot."

"I've got a plan," he said in a rush, desperate to stop the flood before it really got started. "It's a way to keep you around, in his sight, for as long as it takes, it's practically foolproof, and we—we—no, don't do that!"

She had put her hands over her face like a child and began to cry, loudly and without finesse. The force of her sobs shook her slender frame. He pulled her toward him and held her, while gulls wheeled and circled overhead, crying, it seemed, with her.

Much later, the storm had passed and she was left with the hiccups. She pulled back and wiped her tear-stained, puffy face. "I must look gross," she said dully. Had she ever been so unhappy? She didn't think so. Her father hated her. Nothing she could do would make him love her. Nothing. "And you're probably soaked. Hic."

His shirt was decidedly damp at the shoulder but he didn't mention it. "Do you feel better?" he asked, holding her small hands in both of his.

"Yes. A little." Hic. "Thanks for letting me vent. I'm sorry if I made you uncomfortable." She smiled a little and then kissed him softly on the mouth. "You poor thing. You've been through hell these past couple of days, haven't you?" Hic. "First, Sir tricks you into coming to Minneapolis, then he pairs you with a moody virgin, then I follow you to Boston and barge in on your stepfather, who you practically get into a fistfight with, and then you take me to this nice beach and I get you all wet". Hic.

"*I've* been through hell?" He was stunned at her generous nature, not for the first time. "What about you?"

"Oh, well." She shrugged. "I'll get over it. I actually feel much better. I always do when I cry like that." Her eyes narrowed with determination. "If he thinks," Hic. "He can just shove me out of his life, he's nuts. I'm going to stick to him like glue. He's going to see my face every day."

"Attagirl!" Here was the woman he fell in love with, the fearless beauty who had dumped him into Hay Creek.

"But it's not just because of me," she said. Her eyes searched his face. "He shut me out, and that's not so bad, but he shut my mother out, too, and that's wrong. My mother died giving him a child, and he can't forget about her, nor can he shrug off his responsibilities to the child...like he did." Hic. "It's wrong, and he has to know that. Do you see?"

"Yes."

"Sir knew it was wrong and tried to get through to him. But Sir—and I love him dearly, don't get me wrong—but he's...weak. He hates confrontations and he's always had the money and connections to get out of them. He tried for a few days to get through to my father, then gave up, took me, and went away. He made it easy for my father to forget. Now it's up to me to show Brian he can't pretend anymore. He had a wife, no matter how much he wants to forget her, and he has a daughter, no matter how much he wishes otherwise." Hic. Hic. "I'll make him see that, I'll make him acknowledge me and honor my mother's memory, if it takes me the rest of my life."

"You can count on me to help," Erik affirmed. He felt like cheering. She was brave, the bravest person he knew. Damn that man for hurting her so deeply. On the way to the beach, Erik had seriously considered killing him for calling her a murdering bitch. The one thing that held him off was that Stephanie would very probably be annoyed with him if he did it. "In fact, I've got a great plan that will enable you to get into his face all the time, without any trouble at all." He grinned at her. "But I can't tell you while you've got the hiccups. It's too hard trying not to laugh at you."

"I can't." Hic. "Help it. I always get them after I cry hard," Stephanie complained.

"But extremely cute."

"Stop it! I'm too tall to be cute."

"You are cuter than the cutest, most petite woman on the planet. It's not your looks, it's your attitude."

"When did you get to be such an *aficionado*?"

"Are your hiccups gone?"

She paused. Waited for a minute. Nodded. "Yes, I think so."

"Good." He took a deep breath. Looked into her eyes. She looked back, candidly enough, with bloodshot eyes. "Stephanie, will you marry me?"

"Hic..hic..hic..hic..hic..hic," she gasped. "What? Are you" Hic "serious?" Hic! "Is this a joke ?" Hic. Hic.

He silently groaned. Not the most romantic proposal in the world, nor the most romantic response. He didn't know what he expected. Not this. "Yes, I'm serious. I want you to be my wife and I'll tell you why. If you want to hear."

Hic! "Yes!"

He began. This was dangerous territory and he had to be careful not to reveal too much. "You know I'm a little jaded on women in general. I'm not even thirty yet and I'm tired of dating and being chased for my money and one night stands and the whole sickening thing. I liked you the moment I met you, and not just your looks. Everything. You were brave and you didn't care what people thought of your actions, but you were also kind and generous. And you're rich, and your foster father is nobility."

"He's titled," Stephanie managed, still numb with shock. This was a business proposal! He wanted a—a partner, not a lovemate. She didn't know whether to laugh or cry.

"Yes. And I think you liked me, too, though maybe not at first."

Ha, she thought.

"And you're beautiful, too—any man would be proud to have you on his arm. I know that sounds chauvinistic as hell, but it's the truth, whether you like it or not. And I've been thinking it'd be nice to be out of the dating rat race, and to settle down and not worry about who I'd be spending my life with, who would be having my children. And I think you're the perfect candidate. Plus, your virginity makes things easier. I've always been very careful and you haven't had to worry about such things, so we won't have to worry about disease."

"Candidate," she repeated, not quite sure she had heard him correctly. Then, "Disease?"

"Yes. And last—think about it. We waltz into my stepfather's birthday party. Everyone he does business with will be there. People he wants to impress. You and I walk in and I introduce you as my fiancée, and oh, by the way, this is Brian's daughter from a previous marriage."

Against her will, she could feel a smile tugging at her lips. It was true, the image was a seductive one. There was no denying she had been hurt to the core by her father's actions this afternoon. It would be a pleasure to put the man on the spot in front of hundreds of people.

He saw the smile and his heart leapt. She was going to say yes! "What do you think? We can set a date and go pick out some rings this afternoon. We can go see a judge on Saturday—hell, by Saturday night, we'd be man and wife." In all ways. His breath caught as he realized he might very well get to possess that body by the end of the week.

"This isn't just a plot to get me into your bed, is it?" she asked suspiciously.

The woman was a mind reader. "Partially," he admitted with a slow smile. "I have to admit, you've been driving me crazy. I want you more than I've ever wanted any woman. But I have to tell you, it's more than sexual on my part. Truth. In all ways, I find you a refreshing change from just about everyone in my life. You're the woman I want to be my wife. I'm confident we can make it work. The problems some couples have won't be ours. Sir did a great job of bringing you up to be a rich man's wife. And think about the look on Brian's face when we tell him!"

"But Erik—what about love?" Stephanie asked, a little desperately. "I know I must sound naive to you, but I want to get married for love, not to get even with my father or get you out of the dating game."

He went very still. It broke her heart a little to see the wariness on his face. He still doesn't trust me, she thought despairingly. And he wants me to marry him? "Well...I like you a lot, though sometimes you drive me crazy. And I know this marriage proposal probably sounds cold to you, but I wouldn't ask just anyone to be my wife. Really." He smiled a little. "That sounds arrogant as hell. I'm sorry."

She put a hand on his shoulder. "I'm thrilled you asked me," she said. "Really. I know what it must have cost you. Because of your other—because of Margaret. But I've been saving myself for marriage—a real marriage, not just a business relationship. If you and I—I wouldn't be your wife. I'd be your business partner. That's like spitting on everything I've ever stood for, the reason I'm still a virgin at the doddering age of twenty-three."

"But that's what marriage is," he argued, desperate for her to say yes. "It's a partnership. And so what if we're not high school sweethearts, all goo-goo eyed and blind to each other's faults? At least we're going into this with our eyes open. You're well acquainted with my faults, and if I thought you had any I'd know all about them. And— and I'll make you a promise that most men with 'real' marriages never make: I'll never walk out on you and I'll never, never cheat on you. We can put that in the vows or in a prenup if you want."

He looked so fierce, he was gripping her hand so hard, that at first she was so caught up in his expression that she didn't realize he was waiting for an answer. *I love him,* she thought, somewhat amazed that she had been put in such a position. *I love him and I've been wanting*

him forever, it seems. But how can I marry him if he doesn't love me?
How can I not?

"Yes." She took a deep, steadying breath. "Yes, I'll marry you. Yes, I'll be your wife."

He smiled, a big sunny grin that made him look five years younger. "Hooray!" he shouted, pulling her to her feet and kissing her. "Now we'll have some fun."

"I can't believe I said yes," she gasped, wriggling to get free. "I can't believe I agreed to marry you. Three days ago I couldn't stand the sight of you!"

"Yes, it was a whirlwind courtship, all right," he said with mock sobriety, then picked her up in his arms—not without difficulty, she was nearly six feet tall—and staggered toward the water. "But first, the bride-to-be gets dunked."

"Don't you—bllbbphh!" She sat up, spluttering, then went still in total amazement. "It's salty!" she cried, looking up at him with surprise. "It really is saltwater!"

He burst out laughing. "Of course it is, you nitwit. What did you think it was?"

"I've never been to the ocean before," she confessed, standing up and shivering. It was a nice day, but not that nice. "I've only read about it. I knew the oceans were seawater, but it's kind of weird finding out in real life."

"No doubt," he said gravely, then picked her up and dunked her again. She held on long enough to haul him down with her, and in seconds they were both soaked to the skin.

Observers on the beach wondered at the man and woman frolicking in the surf, fully clothed and laughing. September, these observers thought disapprovingly, is not a good time to go swimming on the Cape. They'll catch their death. Tourists.

Much later, exhausted and starving, Stephanie and Erik made their way to the car.

"You're as mean as a rabid dog, Erik Chambers," she scolded. "Hardly the way to treat your future wife, throwing her into the ocean."

His wife. Stephanie Chambers. Or Stephanie Dares-Chambers. He didn't love her—not yet—but he would come around. She would make him come around. He had strong feelings for her, that much was certain, and love would certainly follow.

"Why not? And I remind you that I didn't jump into the water by myself—you pulled me in."

"Only because you dunked me!" she cried, outraged. "Can't you at least say you're sorry? Or look penitent?"

He rolled his eyes at her and unlocked the passenger door. "You're going to drip all over the plush seats in my hideously expensive car," he remarked, unperturbed. "Consider yourself avenged."

"I consider myself unlucky to the extreme." She folded her arms across her chest and glared at him while he circled around to his side. "I must have been suffering from a fever when I agreed to marry you."

"Lucky for me," he said, amiably enough, and started the car. "Do you want to go back to the apartment? Or would you like to see some of the coast?"

"Your place, please. I need a shower. I'm all salty. Then can we eat? I'm starving!"

"Maybe we should find an all-you-can-eat buffet. God help the restaurant you pick."

"I'm tired of going out for supper. I haven't had a home-cooked meal all week," she complained. "Let's stay in tonight. We can cook supper and watch movies and pretend we're a boring old married couple."

"We will never be boring, but if that's how you want to spend the evening, that's how we'll spend it." An entire evening of snuggling on the couch, watching television. How homey. How domesticated. How dull. He couldn't wait.

"Erik, I know we've got a lot of things to get worked out, but there is something kind of on my mind. Can we talk about it right now?"

It would be her virginity, he thought. She was nervous about making love. It was to be expected. He would tell her that he would be gentle, that he would love her, never hurt her. "Sure. What's on your mind?"

"Where will we live? I've got an apartment in the Cities. And Sir's place. And you've got your place in the Cities and, don't you have a home on Cape Cod?"

"Yes. We're only about thirty minutes from there. I'll show it to you sometime this week, if you'd like to see it. But we can live wherever you like."

"You mean it?" Her face lit up. She looked terribly relieved. "But this is your home. You were raised here."

"And you were raised in England until you were a teenager. So why aren't you there?"

She shrugged prettily. He tried not to gape at her curvy, wet body in its clingy wet clothes. "Sir moved us to the Midwest, and we never left. I like it out there a lot. It's unpretentious and the people are nice. And there's space and fields. I miss fields. It's pretty out here, but the trees crowd right up to the road and you can't see anything. I miss being in a car and looking around and seeing for miles. I miss my home and I miss Sir. I'm too old to be homesick, but I am. I know I've only been here a couple days, but I don't think I would want to live here."

He didn't care where they lived. They could live in Africa, if that was what she wanted. "I'll be honest, Steph. I have no happy memories from my childhood on the East coast. If you want to live in Minnesota, that's fine with me; I like it out there, too. But I have to warn you—my business is here, in Boston, so there would be a lot of traveling for me. You might not see me seven days a week."

"But you've got the branch in Bloomington. You could do your business there just as easily. Hire a staff, transfer files, make up new letterhead. It probably doesn't matter which branch you work out of, and if people want you badly enough, they'll come to you. Why did you open it if you weren't going to use it?"

"Good point," he mused. In actual fact, he had opened it so he could see Sir more often. He loved the old man, and wanted to see him more than once or twice a year. And he couldn't marry Sir's ward and then take her far away. Stephanie was Sir's life.

And his. "What would you think about getting a place in Minnesota, and I'll keep my apartment in Boston and the house on the Cape. We can live for a few months in one place, and maybe stay on the Cape in the summertime. I'll use the apartment for business trips to the city."

"That sounds terrific! I'd love to see more of the country. But I'm sure you don't want to neglect your business..."

"My business can do without me for a while. Besides, I could just as easily quit work and live off of your money, isn't that true?"

She laughed. "It is, I guess."

"It's my fate to be a kept man," he groaned. "Just a gigolo for your pleasures. How humiliating. I'll have to resign my membership at the Male Chauvinist Oinker's club."

"You sure will, buster. And one false move and I'll cut you off."

"Ooooh," he leered. "From your body or your money?"

"My money, of course." She was blushing. He loved it when she did that. For all her tough poses, she was very much an innocent. He was only four years older, but his background and childhood had been so radically different from hers that it felt like ten or fifteen.

He suspected she would help him feel a little less world-weary. He suspected convincing her to marry him was the smartest takeover move he had made.

Chapter 15

"YOU'RE GOING to what?" Sir's cultured voice nearly shrieked in her ear. Stephanie held the phone away with a grimace.

"You heard me. I'm going to get married. Probably this weekend. Will you come?"

"Will I—you and Erik—excuse me, I simply must take a moment to mull this over." There was a click as Sir put her on hold. He did that only during moments of extreme stress, like the time she'd called him from the hospital with a broken arm when she was seven. It wasn't her fault she broke her arm. The damned tree branch just hadn't held her weight. But Sir had nearly expired on the spot and came as close to scolding her as he ever had.

"How's he taking it?" Erik asked from the kitchen, where he was putting groceries away.

"Fine," she said, flashing him a big smile.

"Liar," he said, not unkindly. "He's probably flipping out even as we speak. He's got you on hold, right?"

There was a click as Sir picked up. "Stephanie? Hello?"

"Hi, Sir. How are you doing?"

"Fine, fine. I must apologize for my behavior earlier. Terribly rude, do forgive me. Now that the...pleasant surprise has worn off, I must say I'm thrilled. Just thrilled. This weekend, did you say? I beg you to reconsider. Let me throw you a wedding at the house, in a year or so. Enjoy being engaged. We'll invite everybody."

Erik, guessing from Stephanie's bemused expression that Sir was trying stalling tactics, shook his head. Stephanie was pleased. He wanted to get married immediately, no delay. She herself was rather anxious to do the deed, before he changed his mind and decided on another 'candidate'. "No can do, Sir. We're doing it this weekend. We'd really like you to be there."

"Now, you mustn't take this as a criticism, darling, but don't you think you're being a little...hasty? After all, you only just met the man this past week."

"He's the one," Stephanie said stubbornly. "My mind's made up."

A sigh on the other end of the line, fifteen hundred miles away. "Very well, darling. I'll be there tomorrow."

"Great! You can come to Brian's birthday party with us."

"Brian's...ah. All is becoming clear. Yes, I'll be there. You and I have much to discuss." He rang off, leaving a troubled Stephanie with a dead phone.

"He knows," she said, replacing the receiver.

"I told you. He's sharp. He'd figure out the primary reasons for this match made in vengeance."

"I don't care what he thinks," she said stubbornly. "It's his own fault. He was the one who cooked this whole thing up and threw us together."

"That's right. Now come here."

Absently, she went to him. He was sitting on the counter, looking as relaxed as she'd ever seen him. He took her hands and scrutinized them, then peered into her face.

"What?" she said, mystified. He looked like he was going to read her palm.

"What kind of ring do you want? I was thinking of an emerald and diamond engagement ring for you and two plain gold wedding bands for us."

"We need the ring for the party? So let's go shopping tomorrow. Whatever looks good, we'll get. And I like the plain gold wedding band idea, too. Nothing fancy."

Maybe a matching necklace, he mused, his gaze dropping to her white throat. Emeralds set in gold. Or maybe diamonds on a platinum strand. No, she's so pale, you'd barely see the necklace on her. Something with color, definitely.

"Erik? Stop looking at me like that and listen. I agree that we should get married right away, but do you think in addition to a quickie ceremony Saturday, we could go back to Minnesota and let Sir throw us a party? I guarantee he'll be badgering us to let him host a wedding the second he steps off the plane. And I think he's right to make the request."

"Of course he is. He's proud of you. He'll want to show you off. No, I don't mind. I'll tell you the truth, hon. The reason I'm set on a Saturday afternoon 'quickie ceremony', as you so unromantically put it, is because I'd like you to be in my bed Saturday night. Performing the duties of a wife. You're so cute when you go all beet red like that."

"Is that all you think about? And I'm not red, I just feel a little feverish, that's all."

"When I'm with you," he said seriously, "I find it difficult to think of little else. But I'm willing to make a supreme sacrifice. We get the rings, flaunt them at your father's party, and let Sir take a week or two planning a wedding back home. Then we'll get married. Meanwhile, we can make ourselves oh-so-conspicuous out here, dropping by Brian's house to discuss wedding arrangements, giving a press release to the *Globe*—get the picture?"

She nodded enthusiastically. "Promise you won't change your mind?" she asked, suddenly fearful. Here was a perfect chance for him to back out.

"I promise," he said, leaning over and kissing her on top of the head. He inhaled the perfume of her hair for a blissful few seconds, then reluctantly let her go as she turned toward the fridge.

"What's for supper?" she asked, unnerved. He could shatter her calm just by being near. It wasn't fair.

"What do you feel like making?"

She straightened up from the fridge. "What, you think because I've got breasts I'm going to know how to cook? Pig."

"Oooh, you're so sexy when you're angry. And it has nothing to do with being a pig. I don't know how to cook. My stepfather's rich, remember?"

"Oh. Well, so am I, and *I* know how. Shirley taught me back home. I like to cook."

"Little wife," he said affectionately.

"One more crack like that, Chambers, and you'll have your hands full. I can still knock you on your ass."

"You're so adorable, I just can't stand it," he teased, provoking her on purpose. He jumped down from the counter like a cat, all fluid movement and coiled grace. She stepped back, surprised at how quickly he moved, and nearly fell into the fridge. "Oops. Careful, hon, don't want you in cold storage before the big day. Come in here for a minute. I want to clear up a few misconceptions."

He led her into her bedroom. Moving too quickly for her to follow, he flipped her toward the bed. She landed on her back, staring at the ceiling, then bounced off the mattress, kicked off her shoes, and came at him.

"Remember, you asked for this," she said, and flipped him toward the bed in a variation of the move he had used earlier. Except something was wrong. Without seeming to move, he reversed her hold and now she was on the bed again. With company.

"Judo," he said with no small amount of satisfaction. "I've been studying since I was twelve." He pinned her arms above her head and grinned down at her. "I'm not as fast as you are, but I'm stronger."

"Really?" she said brightly, bringing her legs up, hooking them around his shoulders, and flipping him off her. In a second, she was straddling his chest. "Being stronger hasn't done you much good yet, has it?"

He frowned at her. She smiled down at him. And started tickling him in the ribs. He bucked beneath her, laughing helplessly, but she hung on and stepped up the assault. "You're ticklish, I love it!" she shrieked, holding him down with difficulty, her fingers digging into his ribs. "Finally, a weakness I can exploit!"

"Never, madwoman," he grunted, freeing a hand and hauling her off him with no fancy judo moves, just sheer strength. It was about the only advantage he had over her. He held her down with one hand while she wriggled to get free. In a moment, she would be free. "Tickling is for children. I prefer grown-up games."

"Oh, drop dead, you jaded, overgrown, macho—" She went still as he bent toward her, his grip loosening. He locked gazes with her for an electrifying moment, then lowered his mouth to her throat and kissed her gently. All the strength went out of her as his mouth worked its magic and she immediately quit resisting. "You're so good at that," she groaned, cradling his head. She felt his hands moving up, working the buttons on her blouse, spreading it open and pushing her bra out of the way.

"Thank you," he murmured, trailing kisses down her throat and across her breasts. He smiled against her tempting flesh and gently tongued a nipple. She groaned again and he thought he would go mad if he had to wait two weeks, or one week, or one day, or one hour, to have her.

"Your breasts are perfect," he murmured, moving to kiss her other nipple. "Perfect shape. Perfect texture. Perfect taste. I could do this all day. Just...wallow in you."

"I could stand that," she whispered, clutching at him. He pulled her blouse and bra away and kissed her on the mouth, one hand behind her neck, one hand stroking a breast. She put both arms around his neck and pulled him closer, arching up against him as his tongue plundered her sweet, soft mouth.

"Can't we pretend we're married?" he groaned, aching for her so much he could hardly think.

"No!" she said, flipping him away and sitting up. He sat up, too, the shock of being wrenched from her flesh like a bucket of water thrown in his face. "Ha! That got you. You didn't even try to block. All I have to do is get you excited and you're putty in my hands."

"Typical female thinking," he sneered, watching her breasts bounce as she crawled toward him. He flipped her on her back again. "What, you're completely cool-headed after a few minutes of necking? Not bloody likely."

She glared up at him. "Do you mind? I feel kind of silly wrestling with you without my shirt."

"Easily remedied," he said in a voice gritty with passion. He put his hands on her hips, lifted, and pulled her shorts off with a yank.

"Erik!" she shrieked, aiming a kick in his general direction. When the man got excited, he got unpredictable.

"Nice panties," he noted, then pulled them off and tossed them over his shoulder. She was too stunned to resist. "Now," he said, and she didn't like the way his eyes were glittering.

"Erik!"

"Your whole body is blushing. Neat."

"Erik!" She was mortified. No one had seen her naked since she was a toddler. And he was looking at her so strangely, almost as if he were in pain. He reached out a hand that was shaking and smoothed her hair back, his eyes raking her body, drinking her in, and still he looked as if he hurt somewhere. Unconsciously, her hands went to her breasts, shielding them from his gaze. "Erik, stop looking at me!"

"I can't," he said simply, and now his hand was moving down, pulling her arms away. He made a soothing sound in his throat and cupped a breast. He stared and stared at her. "You're the most beautiful thing in the world. And I've never seen all of you before. God, you— you're perfect. Every inch. Look at you."

She squirmed away and pulled the bedspread over her nakedness. He shook his head and grabbed a corner of it. They both pulled. "I am totally, completely, no-question-about-it, not ready for this," she said through gritted teeth, hanging on to the bedspread with all her might. He frowned at her and pulled harder. She hung on, barely. "So back off, buster, or you'll have a real fight on your hands."

"You really are embarrassed, aren't you? Why? Is it because you're a virgin?"

"Of course it's because I'm a virgin, you schmuck!" she shouted, wrenching the bedspread from his grasp. "What kind of idiot question is that? It's also because no one—repeat, no one—has seen me naked since my damned diaper days and you look like you're going to eat me up and we have to wait until we're married so back off, all right?"

"I'll fix it so I can't see you, then," he said with maddening calm. With a casual sweep, he knocked the lamp off the bedside table. It shattered, plunging the room in darkness. "There."

With a final wrench, he yanked the bedspread away and then she could feel his hands on her body, all over her body, she could hear his breathing, harsh and mingled with her own, and she felt his mouth on her neck, his teeth against her skin, and she cried out, excited and afraid, if it was possible to be both at once.

"Shhh," he whispered, his mouth on her throat, on her lips, on her cheeks and forehead and on her lips again. "Relax, love. You know I won't hurt you."

"Quit it," she gasped, even as she reached for his hand and placed it on her left breast. "I'm not strong enough to say no for both of us. And I'm curious and you make me feel so good—but we can't. Are you listening? We can not. Do this. Oooh, don't stop, I like that."

"Your lips say no," he murmured against her throat, smiling. She was trembling beneath him. Not from fear—he didn't think she'd ever been afraid of anything in her life. From something else. "How about this? Do you like this?"

A strangled moan was his answer.

"You're shamefully exploiting my curiosity," she gasped a moment later. She pulled his head toward her so she could kiss him. "Not fair."

"All's fair in love and war."

"This isn't war."

"Do you think it's love, then?" he asked seriously. She went still, so still beneath him, and he was surprised.

"Erik, I—I have something to tell you."

"Please don't."

"No, really, it's—"

"Shhh. Save it for later." She was going to tell him she loved him, and that was nice—hell, it was terrific—but it was for all the wrong reasons. He was making her feel things she had never felt in her life and, in the heat of passion, perhaps she did love him. But he wanted her to tell him when she was cool-headed and in control, not caught in the grip of brand new emotions.

Stephanie shifted uncomfortably. He didn't care. He didn't care that she loved him. Probably an unnecessary emotion to bring to this union. Well, the hell with him. She loved him and she would make him love her and that was the end of it, dammit.

There was a rustling sound that she couldn't identify in the dark—then she placed it; he was taking his shirt off. More sinister sounds in the gloom as he disrobed.

"Erik!" A breathless shriek.

"Oh, calm down. I'm just getting a little more comfortable. And I've left my boxer shorts on, modest boy that I am. I just wish you could see them. They're bright orange with green stripes."

"You liar," she said, giggling in spite of herself. The image of her taciturn love in wild boxer shorts just wouldn't come.

"The wench defames my character! The insult will not be borne." His hands were on her, tickling her ribs, while he bent to her mouth and kissed her.

She ran her fingers up and down his bare back, enjoying the feel of his muscles against her fingertips. He really was a marvelous specimen of a man. She unconsciously scratched him as her excitement mounted, as his hands moved lower.

"That's right, sweet, let me...this won't hurt." Well, it'll hurt me, he thought ruefully. I'm the one who won't be getting any satisfaction this night. But God, am I tempted. It would be the easiest thing in the world to get her so hot she won't refuse me. But she'd never forgive me in the morning.

"We can't," she whispered for what seemed the hundredth time.

"We won't. I won't, I promise. I just want to...I need to do something."

"What?"

"Something you'll like. So you won't change your mind about getting married." In the dark, his voice, usually so strong and arrogant, faltered.

"Erik, you don't have to do anything. I won't change my—oh!"

He wanted her to feel a woman's passion, to find fulfillment. And if she were to reconsider her decision to be his wife, perhaps he could count on her curiosity to make her remain.

He trailed kisses down her breasts, down her stomach. Nuzzled the downy fluff between her thighs, then gently stroked the slick folds, literal virgin territory. He found her very wet, and smiled in the dark.

"Oh, I don't like—I mean I like—what are you *doing*?" His hands were doing such mysterious, wonderful things and she was so caught up in the sensation she forgot to be embarrassed. She clutched at his head, found fistfuls of hair, clung.

"You like? How about this?" And his mouth was where his fingers had been, just a moment ago.

She screamed and nearly leapt from the bed. He held her down, hoping she was more surprised than afraid, and used his tongue as skillfully as he knew how, kissing and licking and gently sucking. In a few seconds she quit trying to shove him away and locked her legs behind his neck. He pulled back and kissed her inner thighs, then nipped her lightly, lovingly.

"Oh, no—go back to what you were doing, it felt marvelous, please, please, please—"

"Shhh. I will in a moment. Are you all right? Are we going too fast? You screamed."

"You startled me," she panted, digging at his shoulders with her nails. "Didn't expect that. And we aren't going fast enough, now will you please finish what you—ah!" His mouth was there, his tongue was there, his fingers were busy and she thought she would die from the sheer pleasure of it all.

"Oh, God, I love—love what you're doing," she managed, nearly giving everything away. That was the last thing he wanted, to be burdened with her petty emotions. He had their marriage all figured out, and it sounded like a fine business plan. But if they would do this, in addition to partnering during the day, she could live without his love being returned. For a while.

"Good. Do you love this?" And he gently, oh so gently eased a finger inside her.

She tried to scream but the sound wouldn't leave her throat. Pleasure was building in her like the sea before a storm. He pulled back and kissed her where his fingers had been a moment ago.

She was shaking like a leaf and making incoherent cries in her throat. It took every shred, every ounce of self control he possessed, not to enter her with a savage thrust and reach his own climax, one-two-three. Her response to him was as exciting as if she had done a strip tease. She was so innocent, so honest in all things, even in her pleasure, and he rejoiced even as he held back.

"I love the way you whimper in your throat like that," he murmured, again easing a finger inside her. "Now if I could only figure out what you're saying." With the thumb of that same hand he gently massaged her clitoris. She went wild, clawing at his back, quivering, calling his name in gasps that sounded as if they were being wrenched from her. He sensed her climax was very near, and was glad, for his endurance was nearly at an end.

Something was. Happening. She was warm, hot, everywhere, but especially where his hands and mouth were, and something was moving toward her like a lumbering freight train, gathering speed as it went, something she couldn't stop, something that might well destroy her even as it fulfilled her.

She cried out again, her throat raw, and he was there, moving up beside her, his hand still busy but his mouth kissing hers and murmuring, "Easy, sweetheart, let it come, shhh, let it come," and she knew he wanted her to accept what was happening, and she tried, but nothing like this had ever happened and she was afraid, she was afraid even while she couldn't wait...

Then it was upon her, an explosion in her loins, fire racing through every nerve ending, and she tried to scream but his mouth was on hers, swallowing her cries even as she realized that this wasn't a scary thing, Erik was here and he wouldn't let it hurt her, and this was a good thing, a wonderful thing. So she gave in, and let the sensations swallow her up, and the world went away for a while.

She wasn't out long, not more than a few seconds. She came back to the world to realize Erik was cradling her in his arms, holding her as closely as he could, raining kisses on her forehead, her cheeks, her mouth. She felt drained and wrung out, as if she had run a thirty-mile marathon. And won.

"Oh, my," she whispered. Whispering was all she was capable of. Her throat was sore.

"Are you all right? You must have blacked out. I thought that only happened in romance novels. Don't scare me like that," he said fervently.

"I'm fine. Tired. Could I have some water?" She would have gotten it herself, except she wasn't sure her legs would support her. The room was lazily spinning. She felt sinfully content and tired.

"Sure, sure, stay right there." He got up from the bed and she sank back into the covers, too exhausted to pull the blankets over her nakedness and besides, who cared? Erik didn't.

"I love you," she murmured to the room and was fast asleep when he returned with the biggest glass of water he could find.

He saw she was asleep and turned on the overhead light to get a good look at her. Even in the exhausted aftermath of violent orgasm, hair sweaty and tangled, face flushed and tired, he found her beautiful. He looked at her for nearly five minutes. She didn't move and he could see she was deeply asleep.

He pulled the bedcovers over her and set about cleaning up the broken glass from the lamp he had dashed to the floor. His hands weren't working right and his legs were trembling. He needed release badly, but he wasn't going to find it this night. She had gotten hers, though, and he was fiercely glad. If nothing else, curiosity would compel her to remain with him until their wedding night. Besides, he was pleased to know he had been the first to give her such pleasure. And what release she had found! He had been afraid the roof would going to come off.

"What a charmer you are," he murmured to her. He noticed that his hands were still shaking. "Sleep tight, honey. I have to take a shower, but I'll be back."

He left the room, walking with some difficulty, and was in the shower for quite some time.

Chapter 16

STEPHANIE WOKE because something was tickling her chest. She stretched to get away from the sensation, but it persisted. Not tickling, exactly. More like—

She opened her eyes. More like scratching, like stubble. Erik's head was bent over her breasts, nuzzling, and when he saw she was awake he smiled and gently took a stiffening nipple into his mouth.

She stretched again, luxuriously, and purred, "Oh, goodie. Are we going to do that again?" She could already feel warmth uncoiling in her stomach and racing down her limbs. His body was draped across hers, she could feel his incredible warmth against her bare skin. She remembered that she was naked and tried to care. It wasn't any good. She liked being naked with Erik, liked the feel of her skin against his. And he didn't mind her state of undress, indeed, seemed to glory in her nudity. At least he had last night. She recalled the look that had been in his eyes and shivered with remembered passion.

"No," he said, abruptly releasing her and rolling away. "I'm already too close to the edge. I was just trying to wake you up."

"What do you mean, too close?" She pouted a little, disappointed they weren't going to continue. She realized she was hungry for him, hungry for what he could do to her. *And this isn't even sex,* she reminded herself. *Wait 'til you get to the real thing!*

He stared at her unbelievingly. "What do you mean, what do I mean? I can't—you can't expect me to—" She sat up, puzzled at his tone and expression, and the sheet pooled around her waist. His gaze dropped to her breasts and he was off the bed and through the door. "Get dressed!" he growled, slamming the door shut so hard it rattled in its frame.

Stephanie heard the shower start up. "Jeez, what a grouch," she mumbled, but her heart wasn't in it. He could put her in a bad mood faster than anyone she knew. What was the matter with him this morning? He was acting like he had when they had first met, abrupt and hateful. After he had been so tender the last few days—and last night!.

She blushed as she recalled how wild she'd been the evening before, how she'd begged him to keep doing things to her, wonderful things with his hands and mouth. It had been incredible. No, not incredible—amazing, mind-boggling. A dozen cliches leaped to her mind, none fit. Pleasure aside, it made her feel so close to Erik, as if they were two halves of the same person. Last night had been one of a kind, and she couldn't wait to find out if the rest of lovemaking was as good.

Erik apparently could, though. He certainly hadn't been willing to get into anything this morning. In fact, he'd gotten away from her pretty damned quickly, as if he couldn't bear to be near her. It was galling. Insulting. Humiliating.

Well, maybe he was tired.

"Or maybe he's just a jerk," she muttered, then got up and went to her closet.

On the other side of the apartment, Erik was reluctant to leave the stinging cold shower. His body ached for release. His pride wouldn't let him tell her how much he needed her, and not just for physical satisfaction. *Good God, you bloody idiot,* he thought with disgust. *Just tell her you love her and you'll do anything for her and let that be the end of it.* Why all this pussyfooting around, all these stupid games of pride? You're supposed to be too old for that garbage. Stephanie isn't like your ex-fiancée, she isn't like your mother, she isn't like her father. She is herself, Stephanie, and the two of you can be very happy together if you get your head out of your butt and tell her the facts of life.

Beginning with how to please a man. Last night had been terrific, but it had also been an exercise in exquisite frustration. He wasn't sure he was up to two weeks of such agony. She could get him excited with just a glance! So what happens when she loses a little more of her shyness about such things and brings her aggression into the bedroom?

"I'm dead, that's what," he said and turned full into the cold spray. His teeth were chattering, he was physically miserable...and still he wanted her. "Gonna be a long two weeks. Me and my bright ideas."

"Him and his bright ideas," Stephanie said, stomping around in the kitchen in her robe and faded bunny slippers. "Let's wait two weeks, Stephanie, then we'll get married. Let's rub your father's face in it for two weeks, Stephanie, then we'll get married. Ha!"

She slopped cereal into a bowl and began eating, neglecting the milk in her irritation. Meanwhile I love him to death and am consumed with curiosity about his body, my body—jeez, I wish we could get married tonight. Then he couldn't wiggle out of it later and we could stop this pussy-footing around.

Stop it, stop it, her gentler self argued. *You're not thinking straight after last night, and his surliness has put you in a bad mood this morning. You love him and that's fine, he'll come to love you after a while. You're curious about lovemaking and that's fine too. But all you've shown him is your temper this week. He's got a lot on his mind, what with your father and you and getting engaged—and don't forget, proposing to you was a big step for him. You don't care, though. All you can think about is what sex will be like. The way you've been acting, it's a wonder he proposed in the first place.*

Well, enough. Give him a smile this morning and show him that there's more to you than the body he adores and the temper he provokes.

"Right," Stephanie said to the empty kitchen. "I always give myself good advice."

That was why breakfast was ready by the time Erik got to the kitchen.

"What do you think? Pretty good, considering I didn't know where anything was. By the way, I broke a plate."

Erik stared at the repast in front of him. She had set the table for two with the nicest china in the house. The roses from last night's bouquet were in a vase in the middle of the table. She had made orange juice, French toast, and bacon for, it appeared, a family of six. The drapes were drawn wide and the kitchen was splashed with sunlight. And she was grinning at him like a mischievous sprite, unconsciously fingering the belt of her robe. "Surprise!"

Erik fought down a shudder. He was not, and never had been, a breakfast person. He was thankful he had perfected a poker face. "Wow! This looks terrific, Steph. Smells good, too."

"Thank you. Have a seat." She took her own advice and scooched her chair up to the table. He took the seat across from her and tried a sip of the orange juice.

"Two or three slices of French toast?" she asked, spatula ready.

He smiled weakly. "It all looks so good, I don't know where to begin. Here, I'll dish myself up. Thank you."

"Welcome." She piled her own plate and fell to with a vengeance. Erik hoped she was so intent on her meal she wouldn't notice he was only picking at his. The smell of bacon grease was beginning to make his head swim.

"Are you mad at me?" Stephanie asked with elaborate casualness. She picked up her glass of juice and drained it in three large swallows. Being nervous always made her hungry.

He jumped guiltily. She had probably assumed he was sulking and as a result, was only picking at his food. To foil her, he took a huge bite of toast and swallowed. His stomach immediately rumbled in protest. "No, of course not. Why do you ask? Mmm, this is good stuff."

"You seem a little touchy this morning. And after last night, the things that we—that I—well, I thought we'd be getting along okay today." She felt herself blushing and was furious. He was going to think her a child, always getting red whenever discussion of their intimacy came up.

He put his fork down and took her hand. Surprised, she dropped her own fork into her plate, where it stuck in the layer of syrup she'd slathered over her breakfast. When he spoke it was slowly, as though he were choosing his words with great care. "No, of course I'm not angry with you. You've done nothing wrong, you never do anything to make me justified in biting your head off...as you always point out. Last night was...unnerving, and I guess that carried over into this morning."

"Is that why you didn't—" She paused, then said it. "Is that why you didn't want me this morning? Because last night unnerved you? Did I do something wrong? I'm so ignorant about this stuff, I don't know anything, I probably disgusted you or something..." Her face was very red, and her breath started to hitch the way it did when she was near tears. She was so angry with herself she could hardly see. *Don't you dare bawl like a baby in front of him,* she commanded herself fiercely. *Don't you dare, don't you dare!* "Was it bad? Didn't you like it? Is that what's wrong?"

"No, it wasn't bad, and I loved every minute of it. I thought you did, too."

"Oh, I did, I did," she cried. "It was amazing. I've had boyfriends, before, but I never let them—is it supposed to be like that?"

"No," he said, "it's usually not that much fun."

"Really?"

"Really. In fact, for me, it's never been that much fun, or that exciting," he said solemnly. "Truth. You were amazing, your body is amazing, your response was amazing—it was fabulous. I wish we could do it all over again."

"Why didn't we this morning?"

"Because," he said, and laughed. "I'm an old man, I'm not up to that much fun."

"Sometimes I think the only reason you like me is because you haven't gotten me into your bed yet."

"But I have." He leered at her, then ducked a flying elbow.

"You know what I mean. I'm embarrassed enough about last night, but to think you didn't like it is awful."

"How could you think I didn't like it? Besides the fact that I stomped into the bathroom after biting your head off this morning?"

He asked the question so innocently, she had to laugh at him, then threw her arms around his neck and hugged him fiercely. "I really, really liked it," she whispered in his ear. "It was amazing! I've never felt that way in my life. Do you think I'm terrible?"

"No."

"Really?"

"Really."

"Good." She smiled at him, then turned in his lap so she was facing him, legs on either side of the chair. She leaned forward and pressed her lips against his, at the same time locking her arms behind his neck.

He was so surprised he nearly tilted backward. As it was, he had barely begun to kiss her back before she was wriggling against his front, creating a delicious friction. Her robe had opened and she placed his hands on her bare breasts.

He groaned mentally. The worst had happened! She had liked what he had done so much she was anxious for more of the same and was becoming as assertive in matters of lovemaking as she was in every other aspect of her life. How was he supposed to fight her off for two weeks? She was such an innocent, she had no idea what a struggle it was to keep from plunging into her lovely body and relieving his frustration with a few well-timed strokes.

He bit her.

"Ouch!" Stephanie jerked back, a hand fluttering to her lip. "You bit me! Listen, jerk, some of your other bimbos might go for the rough stuff, but I'm not—"

He shook her. For some reason, his hands wouldn't let go. In fact, they were stealing around to her breasts again. As a further matter of fact, he was thinking this kitchen floor would be an ideal place for his fiancée's defloration.

He shook her again, briskly, and made his voice sound dry. "Behave. We've got a lot to get done today."

She pouted prettily, but backed off, to his profound gratitude and disappointment. "Oh, all right. Meanie. Let's finish eating, then I'll grab a shower and get dressed."

"After me. I need to take a shower."

"But you just had—"

"I'll be back in a little bit," he said, then made his way to the bathroom, teeth gritted, fists clenched, manhood throbbing indignantly. "Two weeks," he hissed to himself in the mirror. "Your idea, buster, so suffer with a smile. Two goddamned weeks."

"What a weirdo," Stephanie muttered, finishing her breakfast. She'd had no idea he was such a cleanliness fanatic. "Our water bills are going to be sky high."

She was so hungry that after she finished her breakfast, she fell to his.

Chapter 17

"BUT THAT'S THE one I want," Stephanie insisted, admiring the ring on her finger.

"It's a lovely ring," the salesman assured them both.

"It's cheap," Erik protested. "Stephanie, it's less than three hundred dollars!"

"Two eighty-five with our Clearance Sale discount," the salesman said helpfully.

"That's not cheap, Poor Little Rich Jerk, and it's a beautiful ring and it's the nicest one I've seen. Where is it written in stone I have to have a vulgar engagement ring?"

"It doesn't have to be vulgar, but this is so little! Look, you can hardly see the diamonds. Besides, emeralds are your stone."

The trinket in question was a gold engagement ring with a blue topaz center stone. The stone was so cleverly cut that it appeared blue in some light, and nearly clear in other. Surrounding the stone was a circle of small diamonds. It was a lovely, unusual ring.

"I like it very much," she said. "And you've never seen me in emeralds, so how do you know they're for me?"

Erik was in a quandary. Part of him was pleased his salt-of-the-earth fiancée would be satisfied with such an inexpensive ring. Many in her position would soak him for an ostentatious bauble. The other part of him wanted to buy her an ostentatious bauble. He had money and he had finally found someone on whom he wanted to spend it.

"Let's keep looking," he pleaded, ignoring the glare of the salesman. "Maybe we'll find something we can both agree on."

"Doubtful," Stephanie sniffed, but she removed the ring and placed in on the counter. "Thanks for your help," she said to the disgruntled salesman. "We'll be back."

"Doubtful," Erik muttered, and steered her out of the store.

"We don't have a lot of time, you know," she said. "The party's this evening. That's the fifth store this morning."

"Hang the party. I want to get you something gaudy."

"Well, forget it. I don't like gaudy."

"Which reminds me." He pulled her into a lingerie store. "Pick something."

She stood in the center of the floor and gaped at him. "What do you mean, pick something? I don't need—"

"I tore your nightshirt, remember? I want to replace it. So stop staring at me and pick something out."

"Afternoon, ma'am. Sir. Something I can help you with?"

"Yes. My fiancée needs a nightgown. Something beautiful and revoltingly expensive. And we don't have a lot of time, so if you could find her something in the next five or ten seconds I'd appreciate it."

"Certainly, sir," the saleswoman said, smelling money. "This way, ma'am. What sorts of things do you like? Lace? Satin? Both?"

"Actually, I'm sort of a flannel type," Stephanie said, disappearing around a corner. "I had this big green nightshirt that I loved..."

"No big green flannel nightshirts!" Erik called out, ignoring the stares of the other customers.

"I'm sure we can find you something," the saleswoman said doubtfully. "Step in here, please."

Exactly ten minutes later, Erik was handing her his gold card. "Please wait here while I ring these up," she said with a smile. "Your fiancée wants to surprise you with what she picked out."

"I'll bet." He spotted Stephanie hurrying toward him, looking rumpled and hastily dressed. "What did you get?"

"Never mind. You'll see it all eventually, anyway." She'd shopped with abandon once over her initial embarrassment, and was now feeling foolish. He probably wouldn't like anything she'd picked out. Well, maybe that wasn't true. He claimed she looked good in everything. Stephanie guessed she'd find out whether that was true or not.

"I can hardly wait," he said, not appearing very anxious. In truth, the thought of Stephanie in any of the lacy lingerie surrounding them on racks was making it difficult for him to concentrate. "At least you were quick. I've never known a woman who needed less than six hours to pick something out."

"Well, well! I've broken another of your prejudices against women, what a surprise."

He snorted, they collected her bags, and went to eat. After lunch, they headed to Brian Dares' office. The night before, Stephanie had informed Erik she would see her father every day, so he could not shut her out of his mind as easily as he had shut her out when she was very small.

"You don't have to come in if you don't want," she said, stepping into the elevator, pretending her stomach wasn't clenched and her face wasn't pale. Beside her, Erik lounged against the wall and thumbed the Close Door button.

"Don't be silly. I live for confrontations. Besides, yesterday was so much fun, how could I stay away? Here's a kiss for luck. Hello, Kelly."

The receptionist flinched when she saw them. "Hello, Mr. Chambers. Miss Cham—er, Miss Dares. I'm so sorry, but you can't—"

"Kelly, it's going to be very nasty around her for the next two or three weeks," Stephanie said, pulling out her checkbook. "How do you spell your last name?"

"Um. W-I-N-T-E-R."

"Kelly Winter, nice name, here you go." Stephanie ripped the check off and handed it to the receptionist, who looked as though she wished she could be anywhere but where she was.

Working for Mr. Chambers was a literal hell on earth, but Kelly needed the money so she could finish school. She'd been in the man's employ for a little less than a year and went home in tears about one night a week. It's not that Mr. Chambers was such a bad person—well, it *was* that he was a bad person. He was cold and cruel, and she'd quit in a minute if she thought she could make better money in a comparable position. Unfortunately, the money was terrific. Not many receptionists made $28,000 a year, even in Boston. So, for the time being, she was a prisoner of her mediocre business background, doomed to work for this man until she finished school in another three years and found something else.

Mr. Chambers had been like a crazy man when—what was his daughter's name? Stephanie?—when Stephanie had left yesterday. He'd come barreling out of his office, nearly skidding on all the broken glass, and had told Kelly in no uncertain terms that if Miss Dares got past her one more time it was her job. Mrs. Chambers had been in the background, silent for once, just white-faced and thin-lipped, while Kelly stammered her apologies and promised not to let Stephanie past again. Then they'd both left, Mr. Chambers stalking to the elevator like an angry cat, Mrs. Chambers creeping along behind. And the woman *never* crept. Kelly hadn't thought it was in her to creep.

His daughter was so pretty! And she seemed like a nice lady. Kelly didn't understand how anyone, even someone as mean as Mr. Chambers, could try to keep such a lovely person away.

And here she was now, handing her a check.

"This should cover it. Is it enough?"

Kelly glanced at the check and felt her mouth go dry. She had thought in the past that it was a cliché, but all the spit in her mouth really was drying up. She was holding freedom in her hand.

"Seventy-five thousand dollars," she whispered, staring up at Miss Dares the way a puppy stares at a particularly chewy-looking pair of shoes.

"Right. The way I see it, you're between a rock and a hard place. I would guess my father threatened you with dire tidings if you let me in again. I'm sure you have nothing against me personally..."

"No, ma'am," Kelly whispered. Seventy-five thousand dollars! She could quit work, go to school full-time instead of at night, be finished in a year and have plenty left over.

"...but you have to do your job, right? So I'm bribing you."

"Bribing me?"

"Sure. What else would you call it? I'm bribing you to let me in. He'll probably fire you for it and I'd feel better knowing you had something for your trouble."

Kelly stood up so fast her chair shot back and crashed into the file cabinets. She held the check out to her savior. Her hand was trembling. "I can't. It's too much. I'll let you in anyway, but I can't take your money. Thank you anyway."

"The hell you can't." The savior glared at her. *Did I think she was pretty?* Kelly wondered. *She's beautiful. Her eyes are like—like liquid emeralds. Clear and mesmerizing.* Right now they were open wide and blazing at her. "Look, Kelly, I'm loaded. Rich. Grossly wealthy. I spend more than this on clothes in a month." A huge lie, but never mind. "Take the money. It's easy enough to find out where you bank and wire the money into your account. This just saves me some effort."

"I—I—"

"Better give in, Kelly," Erik observed. He was sitting in one of the visitor's chairs, looking supremely bored. He flicked an imaginary speck of lint off one sleeve. "She'll wear you down."

"But—"

"All I ask is that you don't quit. Wait until he fires you. He won't be able to until he has a replacement and that will take a few days. I don't want to have to give seventy-five grand to every receptionist he hires from now until next May."

She could do that. It would be a pleasure to cross Mr. Chambers, knowing she would be safe. And Miss Dares was rich, certainly. Everyone in that family had money. She could afford to give Kelly three years' salary.

"I—yes. Yes. Thank you. This is—you're very kind."

"Not this time. I'm just trying to avoid difficulty. Now excuse me, but I've got to get in there before he hears me and sneaks out."

To Kelly's knowledge, Mr. Chambers never snuck. But, until yesterday, Mrs. Chambers had never crept. Things were definitely turning around.

She watched Miss Dares march in and slam the door behind her. She looked down at the check, then up at Mr. Chambers.

Erik grinned back. Kelly looked as though someone had hit her over the head with the stack of annual reports on her desk. She was still holding out the check. Her hand was still trembling. She was very pale, except for two bright red spots of color on

"Lighten up, Kelly. You don't look very glad."

"I think I love Miss Dares," Kelly said fervently.

He laughed at her. "Get in line."

Chapter 18

STEPHANIE SHUT the door behind her. Her father was at his desk, writing. He didn't look up. His voice, when he spoke, was flat. Almost bored.

"I told you no interruptions. Go away."

"You told me no such thing," Stephanie said, pretending her heart wasn't in her throat. "Well, you did tell me to get out yesterday, but I'm sure by now you've seen the error of your—are you all right?"

His head had jerked up at her words and she watched the color drain from his face, for the second time in two days. His mouth opened and shut and opened again and, for the second time in two days, he could say nothing.

She plunged. "I thought it would be nice if we had some time alone. Without your wife or your stepson. We didn't get much of a chance yesterday."

His mouth was still working. He wheezed. He coughed. He said, "Eh ow."

"What? Speak up, Dad, I can't he—"

"DON'T YOU CALL ME THAT!" His roar filled the office. She had never heard such a sound from a human throat before—all fury and sorrow.

"All right," she said calmly. She pulled up a chair. Sat. Smiled at him. Observed the tic working at his temple. Thought, *I am not going to cry in front of this man.* "What shall I call you? Mr. Chambers seems a little too formal—besides, your name is really Brian Dares. Father sounds awfully stuffy—I suppose I could call you by your first name, but—"

He had apparently gained some control, for he cut across her words in a voice that would freeze boiling water. "I'm going to tell you this once more, young lady, and then you can tell the police. I want you out of this office. I want you out of this city. And if you ever try to see me, or my wife, or my stepson again, I'll—"

"You mean your second wife."

He stopped and stared at her. She looked back, placid as a pond. "Your second wife. What's-her-name. Actually, I don't much want to see her, no fear. She doesn't sound like a very nice lady. Of course, you're not a very nice man, either, but you're my biological father and I have to try."

"Will you quit babbling and say what you have to say?"

"Babbling? Me? You're about as tolerant as Erik, which is just awful. And for your information, I'm not here to say anything. I just have a question."

"I'm not interested in your questions. I want you out of my office."

"Okay. Here it is. What did you do with the money Sir gave you and my mother?"

He had expected something besides that, no doubt, for he gaped at her. She knew by now he had two expressions: the glare and the gape. Time would show her if he had more.

"The money?"

"Yes. He flew to the States when Mama was pregnant with me..." She saw him flinch but went on. "He gave you a big, fat check which you banked for use after my birth. I'm just wondering what you did with it. Did you bury my mother with it? Did you give it to the poor? Is it still sitting in an account in Boston?"

"I used it to start my consulting business." His voice was dry, almost emotionless, but he was trembling. With rage or sorrow, Stephanie couldn't tell.

"Oh. I was just curious. You've done very well for yourself."

"It's easy when you don't have a wife or child to spend money on."

"But you did have a child," Stephanie said gently.

"Sir had my child. He took her. I didn't want her."

"I know." She rose. Checked her watch. "Thanks for answering my question. I've overstayed my welcome for the second time, so I'll be off. By the way, happy birthday."

He said nothing. Just looked at her.

"Goodbye," she said and left.

He stared at the closed door for ten minutes, before he remembered to chew out his idiot receptionist.

"How did it go?" Erik said anxiously as Stephanie emerged from the office. She was calm and dry-eyed.

"Much better than the last time. He didn't throw anything."

"I would have killed him if he had hurt you," Erik said in an icy voice.

"Well, relax. I'm starving, can we get out of here?"

"Sure. In fact, I've got a surprise for you at lunch."

"Oh, good, I love surprises. Can we go someplace that has a buffet? I'm very hungry."

Erik rolled his eyes and moved toward the elevator. Kelly waved them a cheerful goodbye and got ready to face an angry Mr. Chambers. Why he wasn't out here yelling at her already she couldn't imagine.

Chapter 19

THE SURPRISE was Sir, seated at their reserved table. Stephanie squealed and threw her arms around him, drawing the stares of many patrons, while Sir juggled madly not to spill his drink down her back.

"You're here! I'm so glad. Have you ordered? Where's the menu?"

"I am glad to see you, too," Sir remarked mildly, handing her his menu. "You're looking lovely, as always. It must be the glow of the bride-to-be lending such attraction to your features."

Stephanie glowed. Actually, she blushed. "Oh, that. Anything's possible. Why are you looking at me like that?"

"Thinking of another bride," he replied absently, then clasped Erik's hand. "Hello, boy. You're looking well."

"Thanks. You're looking grim. What's wrong, other than our little announcement?"

He waved them into seats and smiled. "Actually, once I got over the shock, I was thrilled. Two of my favorite people, marrying each other. I have always wanted Stephanie to have the best, to find the right man, and in you, she has. I just wish I thought she was doing it for the right reason."

"We are," Stephanie said with a firmness she didn't feel. "We're both adults, Sir, and we know what we're doing. Drop it."

He tilted his head toward her in a mock bow—as much sarcasm as he would ever show—and signaled their waiter. "Consider it dropped," and said no more about the subject.

Much later, after a lunch that the men picked at while Stephanie had three courses, Erik brought up the question on both his and Stephanie's minds. "Are you coming to the birthday party tonight?"

"I don't have an invitation."

"Neither do I. I'm going to crash it. Want to come?" Stephanie asked, green eyes sparkling. "It'll be fun. And with you there, too—I can just see the look on Brian's face!"

"Mmm. Then you'll see the look on the police sergeant's face, after your father calls the police and has us arrested for trespassing."

"Ha! No cop can catch me."

"No, but they can certainly catch me."

"Come anyway."

"I never said I wouldn't, I was just pointing out what might go wrong."

"He probably won't want to lose face with all those people by having the police roust his daughter and oldest friend," Erik pointed out. "But like Steph said, that's a worry for another time."

"Right." Stephanie beamed at Erik and clasped his hand. Smiling, he raised her hand to his lips and kissed it. Sir, who had grave misgivings about their motivations for marriage, felt a little better.

Sir had a chance to capture a moment alone with his ward when Erik rose to get their coats. He leaned forward and said in a low voice, "My dear, I wish you—"

"Can you keep a secret?" Stephanie asked, scooting her chair closer to her guardian.

"Yes, of course." He didn't point out that he had successfully kept a rather gigantic secret for over twenty years.

"I love him. That's the reason I'm marrying him. Not to make my father angry, not for some sort of revenge. I love Erik." Now that it was said aloud, she felt infinitely better. Saying it out loud to someone, even if it wasn't Erik, made it real.

"You do? I mean, good, good. But why on earth is it a secret?"

"Because he doesn't love me. At least, not yet."

"Oh my dear," Sir said, frowning.

"Don't look like that, Sir! I'll bring him around, so just quit it. We're halfway there as it is. He's very attracted to me. And he asked me to marry him, not the other way around."

"Why?"

"He says he's tired of the dating game. He wants to settle down and not worry about such things anymore. And he likes me and he wants me to be the mother of his children."

He was lying, Sir realized suddenly. Or, if not lying, at least not telling the whole truth. The words sounded like Erik, all right, but also like Erik, they skirted around the truth.

"I'm sure you'll be very happy together," Sir said.

"Shhh, here he comes." She shot up from her seat and embraced Erik, who squeezed her back. "Missed you, cutie-pie."

"Save it for your father's party," he said with a growl, then softened the rebuke by tweaking her nose. "There's a present for you up front."

She hurried toward the lobby to see what he had bought for her and Erik pulled Sir aside.

"Erik, I don't—"

"Sir, I know you've got doubts about us, but I can assure you I'll be good to your daughter. Don't look at me like that, you've been like a father to her and I don't care that there's no blood between you and that's all there is to it."

Sir noted that, at times, Erik adopted Stephanie's manner of speaking. "Indeed."

"She's terrific and I want her all to myself. There's more to it than that, I promise you. But I want you to know that I'll never hurt her, I swear on—on her mother's name."

"Well, thank you, Erik. I appreciate that, but I really wasn't doubting your—"

"Will you keep a secret?" Erik looked anxious and glanced over Sir's shoulder to be sure Stephanie was well out of earshot.

"Certainly."

"I love her," he said hoarsely. "I've loved her since I first laid eyes on her, when she bumped her head."

"Bumped her—"

"And even after she threw ice cream on me, I couldn't get her out of my mind. She's so beautiful and good and even kind of innocent, she makes me feel like I could be good, too."

"Well, that's—"

"You can't tell her!" he said fiercely, taking the old man by the arms and nearly shaking him in his determination. "I'll tell her myself when the time is right."

"And when will that be?"

"Right after she tells me. I talked her into marrying me, not for love, but for practicality's sake. I am, after all, a damned good businessman and I still know how to do a presentation."

"Really?"

"Yes. She agreed to be my wife because I bowled her over with my fast talk, but I think I can make her love me. I know I can. She will love me, dammit, and that's the end of it!" He glared at Sir, as if daring the old man to disagree.

"The end of what?" Stephanie asked, staggering under the load of bags she was carrying. Erik, that thoughtful dear, had ordered two lunches to go. He must have noticed the way she had agonized over the menu selections. The barbecued ribs were excellent, and she had enjoyed them very much, but she had been wondering if the French Dip sandwich or the chicken might have been better. Now she could find out.

"The end of lunch, my dear," Sir said with a smile, extricating himself from Erik's grasp with some difficulty. "Let me help you. Goodness! Erik, why did you buy her all this food?"

"I didn't feel like listening to her complain about her empty stomach in an hour," Erik said shortly. "Come on, let's get out of here."

He marched past the two of them, hands in fists at his sides, jaw set. Stephanie watched him go and Sir had time to notice the way her gaze softened before she shook her head. "He has the weirdest mood swings. Don't sweat it, Sir, you'll get used to it."

"Odd. He never had them before. Do you think I might lie down when we return to Erik's apartment? Or perhaps I should go back to my hotel. I'm feeling a bit fatigued after all the excitement this afternoon."

"What excitement?" As far as she knew, he hadn't heard about the awful scenes in Brian's office. Well, he was getting on in years, and was easily tired.

While Stephanie consumed one of the two meals Erik had bought, Sir dutifully admired Erik's apartment and went to lie down in Stephanie's room. Neither Erik nor Stephanie felt it prudent to point out she had yet to sleep there. .

"Thanks again. As long as you keep me fed, we'll have a great marriage."

"Funny, I was thinking the same thing," Erik said, looking at her legs.

"I'm glad Sir is here. I really missed him. I've never really been away from him, did you know? I mean, I don't live in the house anymore, but I could go see him whenever I wanted. I'm glad we don't have to live out here. What do you think I should wear tonight? Should I dress up?"

He was having trouble following the conversation, but he answered that last. "Yes. Dress up. They—he and my mother, I mean— rent one of the ballrooms at the Ritz Carlton. Very ostentatious, overdone affair. I hope Sir remembered to bring his tux. Do you have something appropriate?"

"I guess." She got up from the table and began putting the rest of the food in the fridge. He watched her for some moments, thinking ruefully it didn't matter if she had nothing suitable, she'd still knock everyone's eyes out.

"S'matter, hon? You seem a little pensive."

"I'm nervous about tonight. What if he yells at me in front of everybody and tries to throw me out?"

"Us."

"What?"

"Us. What if yells at us. And tries to throw us out. We're a team now, Steph. What you have to endure, I do, also. Come here."

She went to him, troubled, and he pulled her into a snug embrace. She settled against his chest with a small sigh and smiled as he rubbed the back of her neck.

"I'm glad I said yes," she said. "I didn't think part of our arrangement was that you had to stick up for me."

"Well, it is, goose." His grip tightened until she thought her ribs might crack. "No one would dare speak against you."

"I'm looking forward to our announcement," she said softly, tilting her head back and looking up at him. He looked grave, dark eyes almost black, mouth a thin line. She realized he was troubled over her worries. She forced a smile for him. "We'll knock everyone dead tonight."

"You will. You're beautiful."

"So are you."

He smiled and leaned down to kiss her. Unfortunately, she was leaning up to kiss him and they bumped noses. "Aren't we cute," she laughed, and he kissed her while she was laughing and tickled her until she woke Sir with her shrieks.

Chapter 20

"HAVE I TOLD you how great you look?"

"Twice," Erik replied. "Thank you." He held the door for her, she rushed past.

"Well, you do. Look great, I mean. That tux is dynamite. Black is definitely your color. Boy, I'm a lot more nervous than I thought I'd be."

"Stephanie, do stop chattering. You're starting to give me a headache."

"Et tu, Sir?" Stephanie asked haughtily, ignoring his proffered arm and instead clutching at Erik, who looked amused by the whole thing. His happiness irritated her beyond belief. What was there to smile about, for goodness sake? "And stop smirking, Chambers or I'll smash your face in."

"Such humble words of love. Truly I'm blessed."

"Truly you're a smart ass."

"Stephanie Veronica!"

"Oh, lighten up, Sir. Can we get on with this? Get away from me," she snapped at the coat lady, who scurried back behind her counter.

"Would you like a Pamprin, light of my life?" Erik asked mildly.

"No, I would not. Oh, God, I'm so *nervous*. Is there going to be food here?"

"A buffet," Erik soothed, caressing her bare back. Stephanie shivered at his touch, then instinctively leaned into his hands. He smiled. He didn't think she was aware of her reaction. "You can eat and eat and eat."

Stephanie was wearing a stunning floor-length backless gown the exact color of her eyes. At his request, she had left her hair down and it rippled down her back in glorious blonde waves. Her makeup was at a minimum and the only jewelry she wore was Erik's engagement present.

Just before they left his apartment, he had presented her with a small box. "What's this?" she asked, ripping off the paper.

"Engagement present," he replied easily. "We never did settle on a ring, remember?"

"I remem—oh."

"Do you like it?" He was, to his dismay, more than a little nervous about her reply. He had bought jewelry for women before, but always with an ulterior motive. To get them into bed. To get them out of bed. But this piece he had bought because he thought it was pretty and because he hoped she might like it.

"Like it? Erik, it's beautiful!"

'It' was an emerald and diamond bracelet. Stephanie could only stare at it, agog. It was the prettiest thing she had ever seen in her life. And it was hers. He had bought it for her. And he was looking at her so strangely. It took her a moment to place his expression, because she had never seen that look on his face before. It was hopeful expectation.

"It's beautiful," she said again. Alarmingly, she was near tears. He knew how God-awful nervous she was about tonight and she knew this gift for what it was—a distraction. "I've never had anything so pretty. Thank you. I—thank you." She went to him, smiling, and asked him to put it on for her. He deftly fastened the clasp, then pulled her to him.

"Where's Sir?" he asked pleasantly, cupping her chin in his hand.

"Getting dressed. He'll be ready in a minute."

"Good. Listen." He rubbed his thumb across her lower lip, a lazy smile disguising his passion. His eyes, however, told a different story. "When I take you to bed on our wedding night, this is the only thing I want to see on you. Got it?"

"Yes," she breathed.

"Good." He bent his head and captured her mouth in a searing kiss that left both of them weak-kneed. Sir, frozen in the doorway, had to cough and cough, and finally bang a few pots and pans on the counter before they noticed he was ready to leave.

Remembering the gift and the pleasurable kiss that followed its presentation, Stephanie relaxed a little. Whatever happened tonight, she and Erik had committed to one another. She loved him and he was coming to care for her. In fact, she wondered if he might be in love with her, but too stupid to realize it. It would be like him.

"I need something to eat," she announced.

"I need a drink," Erik muttered.

"It's true, a brandy would go down quite well about now," Sir said. "Perhaps three."

They followed the signs to the party and entered a large ballroom. The room was quite lovely, Stephanie conceded, impressed in spite of herself. Chandeliers, candlelit tables, an orchestra in the corner, and beautifully dressed men and women standing around with drinks in their hands, kibitzing.

It was the kind of party she usually wanted no part of, that usually bored her near to death.

"You know," Sir said, as if reading her mind, "I could never get Stephanie to more than one or two of these a decade. What a charming irony her father hosts such galas three or four times a year."

"Charming isn't the word I'd use," Stephanie muttered, scanning the crowd for the buffet table, and her father, in that order. How could Sir sound so relaxed, almost bored? He had to be almost as nervous as she was. This was a life-long friend he was about to meet up with, after all.

"No. Oh, no."

As one, the three turned at the sound of that quiet voice. Erik's mother stood behind them, pale with shock, eyes glittering with anger. Her hands were clenched so tightly together they appeared bloodless and her lips were pursed as if she smelled something very bad. She looked very much a witch to Stephanie, despite the expensive clothing and pro make-up job.

"You aren't going to ruin his party," she hissed, locking gazes with Stephanie. "You aren't. I won't let you. Just leave. Now."

"For heaven's sake, Mother, is that any way to treat your future daughter-in-law?" Erik said lazily, looping an arm around her future daughter-in-law's shoulders.

"My—what?"

"Erik asked me to marry him," Stephanie said, smiling up at him. "I said yes."

"Erik asked you? *Erik* asked?"

"Yes. You probably thought you fixed it so he wouldn't ask anyone ever again, but he asked me. And I was honored to accept."

"You can't," Mrs. Chambers whispered, raising stricken eyes to Erik's face. "You can't ruin your father's party like this."

"He's not his father, he's *my* father," Stephanie snapped, her temper giving away. "I suggest you get used to it. Give us a kiss." She snatched at Erik's mother and hauled her forward, then planted a sound kiss on the woman's forehead. "I hope we can get along or it's going to be a hellish wedding." She released the woman, who staggered backward.

Sir debated telling the woman that his ward had left a sizable lipstick smudge on her future mother-in-law's forehead. After some moments, he elected to remain silent.

"Mother, get hold of yourself. It's not the end of the world. Oooh, is that Senator Jameson over by the ice carving? C'mon, Steph, I'll introduce you. We'll stop by the buffet on the way over, I promise."

"No!" Mrs. Chambers shrieked. Conversations all around them ceased as the woman became the center of attention. Mrs. Chambers looked around, smiled, then lowered her voice. "You must leave. Quickly. Before I have you thrown out."

"Ah-ah-ah," Erik said, wagging a finger in front of his mother's face, smiling. "My darling is a black belt in aikido and can render your rent-a-cops unconscious without mussing her hair. Do you really want your guests to be witnesses to such a scene?"

"You will not," Mrs. Chambers rasped. She looked as if she would like to strangle Stephanie where she stood. Stephanie almost hoped she would try it. "I'll ask you once more. Please—"

"So, Marcy, who are the newcomers?"

Erik smothered a chuckle. The words were spoken by none other than Mrs. Annabell Lousolito, one of the richest and most powerful women on the Eastern Seaboard. The woman herself had made none of her fortune, but she had married well. Three times, in fact. She was everything Marceline Chambers had ever wanted to be—the richest of society wives, the most well-known and sought-after for favors. And here she was, dressed to the nines, eyeballing his fiancée and obviously dying to know what was going on.

"Annabelle, you old alligator, this is my fiancee, Stephanie Dares, and her guardian..."

"Sir Archibald!" the woman exclaimed. She bent in a deep curtsy, only to be stopped halfway by an embarrassed Sir.

"Please, madam, it's not necessary. Do stand up, ah, there we go."

"Marcy, you sly fox," Annabelle breathed, nearly overcome by Sir's nearness. "You never told me a representative from one of England's oldest families would be here!"

"I—I didn't—"

"Sir Archibald—may I call you Archie?"

"No!" Sir said, actually raising his voice. "Er—that is, I would prefer it if you would use my nickname. Just Sir."

"Just Sir? How odd."

"I gave it to him."

Stephanie stiffened at the sound of her father's voice, so cold and quiet. The man had come up behind his wife, doubtless hearing the commotion.

"Brian! You know this man? And you never said a word."

"We went to Harvard together," Sir said smoothly.

"I married his ex-girlfriend," Brian said, not so smoothly. His voice was ragged, nearly hoarse. He was standing very straight, glaring at all of them. His fists were clenched at his sides.

"So you did." Sir paused, then said gently, "It's nice to see you again, Brian."

"Is it?" the man asked in a monotone. Then he smiled, showing a great many teeth and said to Annabell, "Have you met my dead wife's daughter? This is Stephanie."

"I—I didn't know you had been married before. I thought Marcy—"

"No? Well, now you can tell everyone."

"Brian, please don't," Mrs. Chambers said faintly.

"I don't love my wife," he blurted. "My second wife, I mean. Sorry, Marcy. But then, that's not news to you, is it? No. I used to be in love, but it went badly. She died."

Stephanie spoke up, knowing what was coming. She wanted to beat her father to the punchline, as it were. "I killed her. She died in childbirth. Isn't that right?"

"No," Brian said. For the first time he looked at Stephanie with something like tenderness. Tenderness and a horrible longing. To Stephanie's profound shock, tears were rolling down the man's face. "I killed her."

Chapter 21

"WHAT?" A chorus: Erik, Stephanie, Marcy, Annabell. Only Sir was silent.

"I told you to go away, I didn't want to see you, I *never* wanted to see you," Brian hissed, but now his anger was directed at himself, not at Stephanie. She found herself wanting to go to him, to comfort him, as she had longed to comfort Erik the day they had met.

Involuntarily, she took a step forward. Brian took a step back. She saw this and did not move forward again.

"Why did you come? Why? You know the truth, so why do you want to torture me? Damn you!"

"Hey!" Erik's voice lashed out like a whip. Stephanie shook her head at him and put a hand on his arm as her father raved on.

"I didn't mean to kill her, I swear I meant your mother no harm. I loved her. I loved her more than I loved myself."

"I know," Stephanie soothed, holding up her hands in a gesture meant to placate. "I didn't seek you out to hold my birth over your head. I didn't even know you existed until a few days ago. I know you loved my mother."

"Didn't know I—Sir? Didn't you tell her about me?"

"Uh-oh," Erik said.

"Not...until a few days ago. I couldn't."

"Oh." Brian laughed, a brittle, breaking sound. "No wonder. It's such a pathetically ugly little story. Boy meets girl. Boy marries girl. Boy forces girl to have baby. Girl dies."

"Stop it, Brian!" Stephanie was shocked to hear Sir raise his voice for the second time in ten minutes. "It wasn't like that. Veronica wanted children as much as you did. It was her choice as well as yours."

"No. It. *Wasn't*!" That last an agonized scream as one of the most powerful, ruthless men in America put his hands to his face and sobbed as if his heart would break. "I was wild for an heir. Desperate for children. We started trying right after marriage. Three miscarriages. Three! And I still didn't get the hint. I kept pushing her and pushing her to keep trying to get pregnant. And then we found out the fault was mine—that if I was the father of her child, she would never carry to term. So we turned to donor sperm."

Stephanie thought she might faint. Or cry. Or both. "Donor sperm?"

He wouldn't look at her. He was most carefully not looking at her. "Yes. We matched her with a volunteer donor...and found the two of them to be compatible. So with a little help from some doctors we used his sperm, her egg, she got pregnant...and stayed pregnant."

"You're not her father?" From Erik, who had a pretty good idea who the donor had been. It made sense, but only now that all the pieces were in place.

"No." Still, he wouldn't look at her. "I couldn't give her a baby, so I made someone else give her a baby. I didn't care that technically it would be another man's child. For all intents and purposes, it would be mine and V-Veronica's." She realized that this was the first time he had used his dead wife's name, that even speaking her name aloud after all these years was immeasurably difficult for him. "And then she died. The baby I made her have killed her. My fault. All my fault."

He stumbled past them and, for the first time in his life, Erik put out a hand to steady his stepfather. The man shrugged him off with a snarl and shouted, "Tell her the rest!" before staggering past the crowd of people, his clients and friends and family, who had been hanging on every word.

Dimly, Stephanie realized that no one was dancing. She turned to look at Sir, who looked calm and unruffled despite the circumstances.

"Sir," she said, and then, "Dad."

"Yes," he said. He braced himself for an explosion of rage; he braced himself to be screamed at for a life-long deception and instead rocked backward as she flung herself into his arms.

"Holy God," Erik muttered, putting a hand up to his forehead. He had guessed, but confirmation was another matter entirely. "This is worse than a soap opera."

"Darling—Stephanie, please—your father—I mean, Brian— swore me to secrecy, if you'll just let me explain I'll tell you everything—darling, you're getting me all wet."

"You're my father!" she cried, tears running down her face. "Thank God, thank God—don't you know how many times I've wished you really were my father, not just the person who took care of me when I was little? I'm so happy, S—Fath—Dad—I refuse to call you Sir ever again!"

"As you wish," he soothed, patting her back and smoothing her hair.

Erik went after Brian. He found him almost immediately. The man hadn't had time to get far. His stepfather was in the men's room washing his face, trying to erase all traces of shameful tears.

Erik handed the attendant a fifty and jerked a thumb toward the door. "Out. And keep the others out for a good ten minutes." Then he handed his stepfather a towel.

He took it without seeing, wiped his face, put it down, saw Erik. "Ah, Jesus, what do you want?"

Erik realized at that moment that the man was as old as Sir. He had never looked it before this night. "I wanted to tell you that I take back half the mean things I've ever said about you."

Brian raised an eyebrow. "Only half?"

"You're still a son-of-a-bitch, but at least you had good reason. Besides, I owe you."

"I see. And why is that?"

"I'm still going to marry her. Mother was wrong—we aren't engaged just to make you angry. We're engaged because I can't stand the thought of her with anyone else. But I never would have met her if not for you. So I owe you."

"You sure do. How about dropping a few of your clients my way?"

Erik frowned. "This is no time to talk about business."

"Listen to you," Brian jeered. "She's got you running around in circles so much your eyes are crossed. No time to talk about business— ha! Bite your tongue, boy."

"I'd much rather get back to our earlier topic," Erik said mildly, refusing to let the man bait him. "Your overwhelming guilt, for example, which is completely misplaced and illogical."

Brian flung the towel down and snapped, "Mind your own business, boy. None of this concerns you, so keep your big mouth shut."

He pretended to wipe away a tear. "That's touching. And guess what? All of it concerns me, old man. I'm going to marry one of the characters in this little psycho-drama you've created and we're both tired of lies."

Tired of lies...for some reason, that thought lodged firmly in his brain. *Tired of lies. Okay, how about the lie that you're marrying Steph for her brains and beauty, and not because you love her? There's a lie to be tired of.*

As if his thoughts had conjured her into being, he heard the door open behind him.

"Hello? Brian? Erik?"

"Stephanie, I really don't think it is proper for you to—"

"Oh, relax, Sir—Dad—jeez, this is impossible. The men's room guy is keeping all the other guys out. Hello?"

"Come in, sweetie," Erik said, turning.

"Scram, sweetie," his stepfather muttered, picking up the discarded towel and wringing it in his agitation.

Stephanie walked in, pulling a reluctant Sir behind her. Despite her recent bout of crying, she still looked fresh and beautiful. To Erik, anyway. Perhaps his judgment was clouding reality. Never mind. The result was the same.

"Sorry to barge in, but I'm interested in the rest of the story. Besides, the party got awfully dull after you two left." She smiled at them both, a warm smile that made Erik want to take her in his arms and kiss her senseless. A smile that Brian looked away from, perhaps remembering the grin of a different blonde.

Erik settled for grabbing her hand and pulling her to his side.

"I didn't say a word, Brian," Sir said, fumbling for his pipe, then giving up the search, then fumbling again. "It is your tale to tell."

"Right," Brian said tiredly, daring a glance at Stephanie Veronica. Just looking at her made something inside him hurt. She was the very image of her mother! It wasn't fair. Why couldn't she have looked like Sir? "How much do you know?"

"Let me start from the beginning, please," Stephanie began.

"Do we have to do this in the water closet?" Sir complained.

"No, we don't. In fact, I could use a drink," Brian said, daring yet another glance at Stephanie. It was getting a little —just a little—easier to look at her. She sure was beautiful. All that hair—was it as much a nuisance to her as it had been to his wife? And those eyes—where did those green eyes come from? Veronica's had been blue and, of course, Steph hadn't gotten anything from him. "Let's get out of here and go up."

'Up' turned out to be Brian's suite. Marcy Chambers met them outside the restroom and silently followed them to Brian's room. For the first time since Stephanie had met the woman, she did not look angry or shocked. She was very quiet and thoughtful, and Stephanie resolved to keep an eye on her.

Everyone settled down with a drink in their hand—except Stephanie, for there were no frozen mudslides to be had in Brian's suite. It was just as well, for she was to excited to sit still and paced the length of the room while she narrated the early events of the week.

"...and when he told me that Sir told him my father was still alive—that my father was his stepfather—I flipped."

"She hit me," Erik said to Brian and his mother.

"Right. But you deserved it. So I confronted Sir, who told me that when I was born, my mama died and my father couldn't bear the sight of me; he sold the house and everything else and left the state, leaving Sir to care for me. And when I found this out, I decided to find you and talk to you, Brian, because I thought we should get to know each other."

Brian grunted.

"But you didn't take my sudden entrance into your life as well as I had hoped. In fact, I was afraid you were going to have a heart attack."

"It was a bit of a shock when you walked through my office door," Brian muttered, then downed the rest of his drink in three gulps.

"It certainly was," Marcy said, speaking for the first time.

"Everything Sir told you was true," Brian said tiredly. "He just left out part of the story. Don't blame him for it—I swore him to secrecy. And you know what his word means to him. He couldn't break it, no matter what, no matter how much you may have needed to know the truth."

"I'm not mad," Stephanie said with gentle patience. "I just want to hear the whole story."

Erik, tired of watching her pace, snagged her arm as she moved by him and pulled her into his lap. She wriggled for a moment, then settled back in his arms.

"Okay," Brian said. "When I woke up in the hospital the day after you were born, I knew right away something was wrong. Call it intuition, call it a lucky guess—call it me figuring out I had finally pushed my luck too far...whatever, I knew as soon as I opened my eyes that everything had changed..."

Chapter 22

BRIAN LOOKED around the room. White walls. A sharp, antiseptic smell that told him he was in a hospital. And...cooing?

Sir was sitting beside his bed, holding a baby. His face was lined in sorrow and he looked to Brian like an old man, not the relatively young twenty-nine he was.

"Veronica," Brian whispered. The other bed was empty. "Where's my wife?"

"I'm so sorry, Brian," Sir said quietly and that was all Brian waited to hear. He was up and out of the bed in a single bound, fighting off the remnants of the sedative that left him dizzy and weak.

"Where is she?" he screamed, knocking the empty chair out of his way. "Where's my wife? Veronica? Veronica! Sweetheart, where are you?"

"Brian! Stop this at once! She's dead, she died right after the baby was born. They couldn't stop the bleeding, Brian, I'm sorry, but look! You have a daughter, and she looks just like her mama—"

"GET HER AWAY!" Brian roared, backing away from the small bundle like it had the plague. "Oh, God, that thing killed my wife. My wife is dead! Oh, God, why didn't I listen? Why did I make her have a baby? Oh, please, Sir, tell me I'm dreaming. Please, she can't be dead! Please! She was the only good thing I had! I didn't mean to kill her. I didn't mean—"

Sir, maneuvering away from Brian with the child in his arms, the child that for some reason wasn't crying at the top of her lungs despite all the shouting, managed to press the button to summon a nurse. Brian needed to be sedated again, and quickly.

"Brian, listen to me. Listen. This baby didn't kill Veronica, any more than you did. It just...wasn't meant to be. That's all. It just—"

"That's all? That's *all*? My wife is *dead* and you're telling me it's no big thing? God damn you both." His voice broke as he flashed back to their wedding night, when Ronnie had smacked him on his bare ass with her hairbrush, laughing like a loon while he chased her around their suite. "Oh, Ronnie. I'm sorry, love, I meant you no harm."

Sir tentatively tried to show Brian the baby, but Brian wouldn't look. In fact, he moved toward the door and said in a thin, dead voice,

"Get it away from me or I'll crush its head."

That was the last time Sir tried to show Brian the baby. In fact, Brian never actually saw the baby—just a small lump in pink blankets.

Much later, after the house had been put on the market, after Sir had named the baby, after Brian had begun the spiral into the ruthless business man that would shape another child to be as grim and unloving as he, after all this, Brian came to see Sir.

"Don't bring the baby out. I don't want to see it. I wanted to talk to you before you left. You're going back to England?"

Sir, shocked by Brian's appearance, could only nod. The man appeared to have lost twenty pounds in three weeks. He looked like a malevolent scarecrow. An old malevolent scarecrow.

"Good. I don't want to see you anymore. You're my best friend, Sir, but I look at you and I remember the three of us at school. God, she was a bookworm. I had to teach her to have some fun."

"She was very studious. That's why we broke up. But she put books aside for you. She loved you, Brian."

"Yes. And look where it got her. In a hole about six feet deep and six feet long. The sooner you're gone, the sooner I can put this shit behind me."

"You will never be able to put it behind you until you forgive yourself."

"Sure I will. I just won't think about any of it, ever again. I can do it, too. You watch."

Sir said nothing.

"Besides, it's right that you should take her. She's your daughter, after all."

"She was meant to be yours and Veronica's. I wouldn't have insisted on raising her if you had wished to take responsibility."

"Well, I don't wish it," Brian grated. "I don't wish to see her again, ever. Let me just say what I need to say and then I'll be out of here."

"Very well."

Brian took a deep breath. "I don't want you to tell her the truth about her origin. Tell her you were friends with her parents and they were killed right after she was born. Tell her that."

"But why? I don't—"

"Just *do* it!" Brian screamed, and in the other room, a baby began to cry.

"Calm down. I would hear your reasons."

"Technically, she's a bastard, you English prig. Her father and her mother weren't married. I don't care how modern people try to be, I don't care about the claims of science, that someday every other baby will be the product of donor sperm, I won't have any child of Ronnie's wear that stigma. That's one reason."

"And the other?"

"I don't want her to hear that I used her as an instrument to kill her mother."

"What?"

"You heard me. I was so crazy to have a baby, I talked you into being a donor and the baby killed Veronica. Do you think she'll be pleased to hear that? Hell, no. So she won't hear it, not ever. Clear?"

This was a stranger. This wasn't Brian Dares, classmate chum, old friend, endless tease and die-hard practical joker. This man before him was no one he knew. He didn't even sound like Brian Dares.

"I'll have your word on this, Sir. It's the least you can do for me. Your word that you'll never tell her you're the father."

"I'll never tell her I'm her father." About the rest, we'll see, Sir thought.

The baby's crying escalated and Sir turned in that direction. When he came out, carrying Stephanie in his arms, Brian was gone.

Brian was gone, but he had Stephanie. Stephanie Veronica Dares. His daughter, though he had put Brian's last name on the birth certificate.

He was a father, though no one must ever know. His daughter would know him as a family friend, a guardian, nothing more. It was what Brian wanted, so it was what Sir would do. It might as well have been a last wish. The Brian he knew died when Veronica was wheeled into the morgue.

He looked at the small bundle in his arms. Stephanie was remarkably beautiful for a newborn. Her skin was clean and pink, her eyes a clear blue that he knew would darken into anther color, although which one it was too early to say.

"And what are we to do with you, my dear?" he murmured, and shut the door behind Brian.

Chapter 23

"WHAT HE DID was raise me as best he could," Stephanie said, favoring Sir with a warm smile. She went to him, put her arms around him. "You raised me and took care of me and gave me everything I needed and almost everything I wanted and kept a bunch of pretty big secrets and I love you so much I think I'm going to make a fool of myself."

"I love you too, Stephanie. From the moment I laid eyes on you."

"Do you think you can't love me? Or did you never try?" Marcy asked suddenly.

"What?"

"You heard me, Brian. Are you unable to love me or unable to make the effort?"

"Well, I—uh—"

"Because I would like to try. I am quite fond of you, you know. I married you for your money, to be sure, and there's certainly a lot of that, but for all your gruff posturings you've given my son and me a good home. And I am tired of the mistresses."

"There's only one now," Brian said absently.

"A good home?" Erik yelped. "Mother, he was an insufferable jerk most of the time!"

She ignored her son; all her attention was on Brian. "I would like to try."

"Marcy—"

"Marceline. How many times do I have to tell you? Marceline."

"Sorry. Marceline, I can't promise you anything. I haven't really come to terms with Veronica's death yet, and—"

Stephanie pulled away from Sir and went to Brian. "Stand up," she ordered in a gentle tone.

He stood, inwardly grimacing. He knew a hug was coming and, while he appreciated the sentiment, he was uncomfortable with displays of emotion, even among family.

She poked him in the stomach. The breath went out of him with a whoosh and he bent over.

Erik burst out laughing. Finally, he thought. The bitter old bastard's had that coming for about twenty years.

"That's for taking yourself too seriously," Stephanie said. "Am I like my mother?"

"Yes," Brian gasped, straightening.

"Well, then. Do you really think Mama would let you talk her into anything she didn't want to do? Or is it too convenient to take all the blame? She died, Brian. Awful as it is, these things sometimes happen. It wasn't your fault. It wasn't Sir's fault. It wasn't my fault. She died and she's in a better place now, and she's been watching you torture yourself for the last twenty-some years and she's really pissed at you, I bet."

"I never thought of it like that," he wheezed.

"Be fair, Brian. You never thought of it, period. You just took all the blame on your shoulders and that was that, as far as you were concerned. I've heard the whole ugly story and I don't blame you. Do you think Mama does, wherever she is? The only thing we can blame you for is making yourself miserable for two decades. For a Harvard grad, you can be awfully dumb sometimes."

"Thank you," he said, feeling oddly content.

"Welcome."

"Marceline, we can try, but you're nothing like Veronica. I don't know if I can love you."

"I don't want to be like Veronica. All I want is an effort to be made."

Erik shook his head. He supposed it was understandable that his mother was tired at long last of her marriage of convenience, that she wished for something besides a checkbook for her old age. It was understandable, but he had trouble believing it. His mother had unwittingly helped him shape his views about women, and if she was changing her ways, what did that tell him?

"I think I need another drink."

"I think I need all of you to get the hell out of my suite," Brian said tiredly. "I'm glad we're all friends now, hip, hip hooray, but I'm beat. We can get together tomorrow and expound on how wonderful it is that we've found each other."

"You've got a party to get back to, buster. Your birthday party, remember? I imagine Annabell is dying to hear what went on in here," Marceline said.

"She can read about it in the papers. I invited enough reporters tonight and I'm sure they caught the whole lovely scene. I'm going to be very angry tomorrow morning."

"I look forward to it," Sir said smoothly, rising. "We will take out leave of you, Brian, but I would like to see you tomorrow."

"All right. Hey! When's the wedding?"

"Two weeks from tomorrow," Stephanie said and Erik silently groaned. "In Minnesota. We decided to let Sir throw us a party. Will you come?"

"Yes," Marceline said firmly. "After all, my son is marrying an heiress. It will be quite an event and we wouldn't miss it."

"Glad I've got your approval," Stephanie muttered. She still didn't care for Erik's mother. True, it was unfair to hold past actions— actions she hadn't even witnessed—against someone, but she couldn't help it. Marceline Chambers was a bit too mercenary for her taste. "'Bye."

Sir checked into the Ritz, while Erik and Stephanie took a taxi. Stephanie chattered all the way home, excited over the evening's events, and Erik did his best to listen, but he loved her and wanted her so much it was difficult to hide his feelings. As a matter of fact, as each day passed it grew more and more difficult to restrain from declaring his love and making himself vulnerable to her.

Business arrangement, he told himself. That's the track you took with her. You're getting married to get out of the dating game. She's the most qualified candidate.

"And Sir is my father! Oh, Erik, do you know how happy that makes me? Nothing against Brian, you know, but I love Sir so much and he took care of me and it's only right that he get the credit, right? This was the most exciting night of my life!"

What about the day I proposed? he thought forlornly, if a little unfairly.

This had to end. But he was still too cowardly to take the step, to expose his soul, to make himself vulnerable. He was afraid and despised himself for his fear.

Chapter 24

LATER, ALONE in the guest bed, Stephanie's thoughts ran in the same direction. Erik was still in the livingroom and she could certainly take a hint. She'd gone to her lonely bed, not even bothering to ask him to join her. And there she remained, her thoughts whirling.

The amazing part of it was, Erik filled her thoughts far more than the recent revelations did. Her life had changed dramatically in only a few days. And she had a big step coming up—a wedding, a marriage. And she still hadn't dared tell her groom she was hopelessly in love with him.

What a mess, she thought and it was a long time before she fell asleep.

Erik, trapped with his thoughts in the living room, finally fell into an uncomfortable doze, slept restlessly, and was up just after seven a.m.. He stumbled into the bathroom only to find that Stephanie had beaten him there.

"Morning!" she shouted over the pounding of the shower. "I'll be out in just a minute."

"What are you doing up so early?" he asked dumbly, staring at her outline through the nearly-opaque shower doors. He couldn't make out anything tangible...just maddening shadows and curves.

"Couldn't sleep. What should we do today? Want to go sight-seeing?" The shower shut off, she opened the door a crack and smiled at him. "Would you hand me my towel?"

Like a sleepwalker, he shuffled over to the rack, retrieved her towel, handed it to her. She stepped out, wrapping it around herself, and bent toward him for a kiss.

He leapt back, nearly cracking his skull on the open bathroom door, and stammered, "I have to go into the office this morning. I'll take you sight-seeing this afternoon."

"Oh. Okay. I guess I can putz around here for a couple hours," she said cheerfully, moving toward the mirror. She put an arm up to wipe the cloudy surface and her towel slipped. With a muffled groan, he fled.

Erik prowled the living room like a caged panther. This was going to be harder than he thought. The woman obviously had no idea how strongly the sight of her glorious, beautiful, flawless body affected him.

And why should she? She was an innocent. It was one of the things he liked about her. And it was clear she trusted him implicitly, else she wouldn't be running around his apartment half-clothed. These things warmed him while at the same time they dismayed him. He wished she was a little more aware of her sexuality so she would realize how she was torturing him.

He fled the apartment as soon as he could, hid at the office as long as he dared, and returned to his apartment with heavy feet. His employees had all heard the news of his engagement and were full of praise and congratulations that he barely heard. Part of him was pretty darned happy that, if he wished, he could pack everything up and live off of Stephanie's money. He wasn't likely to do that, but it certainly took some pressure off. All his life he had worked hard and he was proud of the money he had earned. Still, knowing he had the option of blowing off the office for months at a time was attractive. He had never much cared for his work. It was something that made him a lot of money and paid the bills. But now, things had changed. If he didn't wish to keep his office open, he didn't have to. Hell, just the thought of all the time he and Stephanie could spend together brought a smile to his face.

A smile that was quickly wiped off when he walked into his living room. Stephanie was reclining on the sofa, reading one of his books. She jumped up when she realized he was in the room and he stifled a groan.

"You're home! Terrif! Oh, wait, I'm doing this wrong." She stretched up on tiptoes and kissed his cheek. "How was your day, dear?"

He was numb. He didn't even feel her lips. She was wearing a little nothing from Victoria's Secret. How much had he spent? How many things had he bought? He couldn't remember.

She walked away from him and his eyes were drawn to her tight, round buttocks and narrow waist. Considering the fact she didn't spend eight hours a day in a gym, she was in superb shape. Must be from all the trout-fishing and cow dodging she had done in Minnesota.

"That's nice, what you've got on." His voice sounded strange, like he was choking. He cleared his throat. "Why don't you get dressed? I'll take you to Fanueil Hall."

"Okay," Stephanie replied. "I'll just pull some shorts over this and we'll get going. What's Fanueil Hall?" That last over her shoulder as she disappeared into her bedroom.

That was all she was going to do? Pull shorts on over that little lacy thing? It covered her decently enough, but it was so damn clingy...you could see every curve. Was he going to spend the day in heat for his fiancee? Or fighting off would-be Romeos?

"Christ," he muttered, flinging his briefcase aside with a snarl. It crashed into an end table and he felt a little better.

In her bedroom, Stephanie heard the crash and snickered. Prideful, foolish man. She loved him, but she was certainly enjoying this. And my! Hadn't his eyes popped out when he saw the latest instrument designed to bring him to his knees? Well, she wasn't sorry. He had it coming for denying both of them and for keeping what was in his heart to himself.

Aarrgh! Who was she to be so smug? She was guilty of the same thing. And really—what was the big deal? Three stupid little words. And if he can't say them back right away, is that so awful?

Yes. Nevertheless, Stephanie was tired of the constant circle, tired of being a coward, and just as tired of his cowardice.

She realized with an unhappy start that if she could have left him without being miserable the rest of her life, she would have. Unfortunately, it was far too late for that. Plus, emotions aside, she couldn't see any other man taking her virginity. In fact, the thought of someone else doing that to her made her shudder. She was stuck with him, and he with her.

She pulled on her shorts, slipped into a pair of flats, grabbed her purse, and hurried back to the living room, a determined smile on her face.

"Let's cruise, baby," she said. He nodded mutely and held the door for her.

In the elevator, she ignored the leering attendant and said, "Have you thought about the marriage vows?"

"What?" He had been thinking that if he pleasured her enough, she might say the words. This time, he wouldn't shush her. He would welcome her declaration, even if made in the throes of passion.

"The vows. You always keep your word, right?"

"Right," he said firmly, having no idea what she was talking about.

"Well, we have to promise to love and honor. And since this is a business arrangement, we'd be lying. So what are we going to do? Lie? Or should we change the vows?"

Damn her. She could talk about lying and vows and love and honor with that silly smile on her face, never knowing how she was twisting the knife in his guts.

He was suddenly furious—with her, and himself, and reacted the way he always did; by taking it out on someone else. "If you don't stop leering at my fiancée, you putrid little creep, I'm going to beat the shit out of you."

"Hey!" Stephanie said angrily. "If anyone beats the shit out of him, it'll be me. I'm the one he's been looking at."

"I'm s-sorry, Mr. Chambers," the attendant stammered, backing up against the wall. Everyone in the building knew what a bastard Mr. Chambers could be when he was riled. Oh, he'd done it now! But could anyone blame him? Mr. Chambers' fiancée was a real piece of work. So tall and pretty and all that hair...

"Don't you dare apologize to him! Apologize to me if you've a mind to. I'm the offended party."

"S-sorry, Mrs. Chamb—Miss Stephanie."

"Well, it's no big deal so just relax. Really. You're all scrunched up against the wall. And forgive my doltish fiancé for being such a dork. Hey!"

The elevator doors had opened and Erik stomped out, leaving Stephanie yakking with the attendant. She ran after him.

"Hey! Wait up, jerk!"

He slammed through the doors without breaking stride and turned up the street, forgetting, in his anger, the cab he had called.

A piercing wolf-whistle split the air and he turned. Stephanie was just taking her fingers from her mouth when he said, "What a disgusting talent. Don't do it again."

She smiled at him, her sweet smile, and promptly whistled once more, this one even louder than the last. Nearly everyone on the street was staring at them, except for the two homeless men sitting on the bench opposite them. They were trying to whistle the same way, fingers in their mouths, and failing.

Stephanie hurried toward them. "Your fingers are too close together," she told the homeless men. Then, to Erik, "If we're going to be married, I suppose I'll have to get used to your dumb mood swings."

"Dumb? Mood swings? I'm as steady as a rock," Erik said, glaring.

She glared back. "You're as steady as sand on the beach. What's the matter with you?"

"You." He nearly bit his tongue at the look on her face. "I didn't mean that." He did, but not the way she was taking it. "It's...I have so much work to do. I don't really have time to play tour guide. Maybe...maybe you'd better go back home for a while."

"I see," she said carefully. Her face burned with humiliation. "Well. I have *no* interest in remaining where I'm not wanted, I assure you."

He rubbed his eyes, hard. *Aw, shit.* "Stephanie...it's...none of this is your fault."

"No, of course not, I'll blame the dog," she said coldly. "And you don't have to worry. I'd never dream of keeping you from your work. I'll go back to Minnesota, and you can join me on our wedding day. If you can get away from the office, that is, and if you still want to be married, which right now I very much doubt." She ignored his flinch. "And you'd better think about whether or not you want to be tripping over me the rest of your life. If my continued presence is going to be a problem, let's call this 'business deal' off." She spun and marched back into the building.

He groaned and raced after her, seeing her red face just before the elevator doors closed. Foot tapping, he waited for the next one. He wasn't about to climb fifteen flights of stairs, although in books the hero never hesitated to pound up umpteen flights after his ladylove.

He got to his apartment seconds after she did and found her throwing clothes on the bed and hunting for her travel bag at the same time. Her hair had pulled free from its ponytail and was hanging in her face. Impatiently, she blew it back from her forehead.

"Can I—uh—are you sure you want to leave?"

She looked at him incredulously. "You're the one who asked me to leave, Chambers."

Don't go. I can't live without you. He opened his mouth, but what came out was, "Sir is still here, we're supposed to have dinner with him tonight. And you're just going to take off without saying anything to Brian?"

"Why not? It's not like he's my father or anything. Besides, I'll see him at the wedding. Your treacherous mother will make sure they're both there. Assuming there is a wedding."

"Don't talk like that," he said sharply.

"Oh, right. Sorry. I know how you panic when a deal is about to fall through."

"This is a little more than a 'deal'," he snapped.

She raised her eyebrows at him. "Is it?"

Silence. She shrugged and turned back to her suitcase. "This is just so you know: you can't be a jerk, and say mean things and behave badly, without paying some sort of consequences. I can't keep forgiving you and forgiving you, only to have you walk all over me a few hours later. Call me a cab on your way out," she said.

"Fine," he said, dying inside.

"Fine."

"See you in two weeks."

"I guess that's up to you," she said distantly. "Go call me a cab."

He hesitated, as if he wanted to say something, then turned and left. She willed herself not to cry, but it was a close thing. Her anger and humiliation were very great. And she wasn't just angry at him. This whole mess was of her making. She'd agreed to marry a man she knew didn't love her. She kept expecting him to act like a man in love, and kept getting hurt when he wasn't able to comply. So who was the idiot?

She wasn't sure, not anymore, not about anything. All she knew was that he wanted her gone, and so she would go.

She finished packing in record time. He was waiting in the living room and stood as she lugged her travel case down the hall.

She shook her head at him as he moved toward her. He stepped back and they parted without a word.

Chapter 25

SIR CAME home to find his daughter on the floor in one of his living rooms, surrounded by what appeared to be three dozen bridal magazines. She was cutting out dresses and muttering under her breath.

"Good day, my own," he said, pulling out his pipe and searching his pockets for tobacco. Behind him, the chauffeur moved toward the stairs with his bags.

She looked up and smiled, but he noticed the worry lines etched in her forehead and around her eyes. "Hi, Papa."

"Papa?"

"I'm experimenting. How about Padre?"

"What's wrong with Sir?" he whined.

"Forget it."

"We'll settle on something, then. I seem to have interrupted your work. Forgive me."

"Don't sweat it. I was getting ready to call it quits, anyway. I'm going buggy looking at all these pictures."

"May I ask what you're doing?"

"Nothing important. Did you see Erik before you left?" This in an absurdly casual tone, as if she were asking about the weather.

"Yes, I did. He met me for dinner and explained your absence."

"I'll bet. Did he tell you it was all his fault?"

"Yes."

"What?" Stephanie felt her jaw drop. With an effort, she shut her mouth. Sir, unruffled as ever, began filling his pipe.

"He told me he behaved badly, offended you, and you left. Then he apologized for your absence. Then he got drunk."

"Erik...got drunk?"

"It was quite amusing." He smiled at her, a little cat smile that had always irritated her to no end. "He's quite enamored with you, I think."

"Well, you think wrong," Stephanie snapped. "And I'm beginning to think I should ditch him and get on with my life." She held up a fistful of magazine cut-outs. "What do you think of these dresses? Oh, and I want tulips for my bouquet. Lots and lots of tulips. Red, okay?"

"In September?"

"So find a greenhouse."

"As you wish. May I ask why you're considering calling off the nuptials? Yes, that looks fine—maybe in a nice ivory?"

Stephanie squinted at the cutout, then at Sir. "Huh? Oh. I don't know. I'm not sure if I can live with him and his mood swings. And he's mean to me when he's in a bad mood. You think ivory?"

Sir coughed politely. He loved Stephanie, but living under the same roof with her had always been a trial. A loud trial. He thought Erik would have more difficulty living with Stephanie, rather than the other way around.

Stephanie picked up another magazine and began leafing through it. "Did you see Brian before you left?"

"Yes. He and his wife, Marceline. She seems to be making a determined effort to win him over. I hope it goes well. He could be happy now that he's letting himself acknowledge what happened."

"What about you?" Suddenly shy, Stephanie looked at him through a curtain of hair. "Will you be happy now, since the truth is out?"

"I have never been unhappy, dear," he said mildly. "I have always known that I was your father. And you have always thought of me as a father. The only thing changed is that you know it's true in blood as well as in spirit."

"Oh. Well, good. How's Brian doing?"

"As well as can be expected. He was disappointed you had left for the Midwest. He wanted to see you again."

"I'll bet."

Sir frowned. "No, I think it was a genuine wish on his part. Now that the truth is out, things are easier on him. You remind him of Veronica, but that is beginning to seem, I think, a blessing instead of something that hurts. He and Erik have even come to an amicable agreement. As I recall, they were planning to collaborate on a few business ventures when I left."

"Mmm. By the way, you're giving me away."

"Yes."

"Assuming I don't call it off."

"Of course. May I ask why you're considering it? Politically and economically, it's a good match. You could certainly do worse."

"Sir, please! This is the twentieth century. People get married for love—or they ought to—not because it's a good match."

"Ah."

"I don't think I can make him love me back, that's all," she said in despair. "I thought I could, but...and if I can't, I don't want anything to do with him. I'm not going to spend the next few decades hopelessly in love with a man who couldn't care less. You think I want to end up like Marceline?"

"What makes you think he doesn't love you?"

"He sent me away. He said he didn't have time for me."

"You have never told him, either. And as for your talk about love, I remind you that ten days ago, you had not yet met the man. You haven't given him time. Why do you assume he *meant* for you to leave?"

"Because he always tells the truth," Stephanie stammered, thinking hard. Except, she remembered, when confronting his feelings about me. "He's honest. That's what I meant."

"Yes. Exactly as honest as you in this matter. You cannot expect him to read your mind, dear one. Have you thought that he sent you away out of frustration?"

Yes. Sexual frustration. Stephanie kept that thought to herself. "I don't care why he sent me away. I just know that I hated it."

"Then why did you go? You were never one to obey when it wasn't your wish."

"Because...because he hurt my pride. And I didn't want to spend the last two weeks hanging around, wondering if he wanted me near him or not." She sighed. "I suppose...I suppose I should have calmed down and tried to talk with him like a sane human being."

"Indeed." He took a pull on his pipe. "What color tulips? Red?"

"Yes. Lots. Can we get this together, please? We've only got ten days or so."

"You will have anything you want, in any quantity you want. Just let me know."

She sighed again and looked at the litter of magazines surrounding her. Sir couldn't get her what she really wanted, which was Erik's undying love. Well, red tulips were a start.

Chapter 26

IT WAS THE longest two weeks of Erik's life. Every day he replayed the last argument they'd had. Every day, he saw ways he could have shut his mouth and not hurt her. Every day, he thought about calling her and apologizing, and every day he chickened out. In truth, he wasn't ashamed of apologizing for his boorish behavior, he was afraid that she might tell him the wedding was now off.

He flinched whenever the phone rang and kept the machine on to screen all calls. She never called with a cancellation but that didn't stop him from worrying. The days crawled by, with never a word.

Finally, it was the Friday before his wedding day. He had been packed for a week and was at the airport three hours before his flight left. He had a bad moment when he thought he had left her wedding present at the apartment, but after opening his suitcase in the men's room and digging through his clothes, he found it.

By the time the plane landed at the Minneapolis/St. Paul International Airport, he was a nervous wreck. He had been driving his seat mate crazy for over an hour with his practicing. "I love you, Stephanie. Stephanie, I love you. I love you, Steph. Stephanie, I love you. I love you."

When he saw she was waiting for him at the gate, he froze. The man walking behind him, his long-suffering seat-mate, slammed into his back, but Erik hardly felt it. He tried to look nonchalant as he practically ran to her side.

"Hi, beautiful," he said casually. "Been waiting long?"

She frowned at him. She was wearing ripped jeans and a ratty sweatshirt. Her hair was pushed up under a filthy baseball cap. He recognized it as the one she wore trout fishing.

Beautiful? Stephanie wondered if he was teasing. She had deliberately worn her grossest clothes. "A couple minutes," she lied. Actually, she'd been here for over two hours, worried his plane might come in early and she would miss him. "Come on, let's go get your bags."

"Wait a minute," Erik said, catching hold of her elbow. The contact was electric. Stephanie shivered and he had a moment when he couldn't swallow. *My God,* he thought. *I'm grabbing her elbow, which* is clad in a fishy sweatshirt, and I want nothing more than to lower her to these hard plastic seats and love her for hours. "About the other day—our argument. I—"

"It doesn't matter," she said, shrugging. "Let's just forget it."

He grinned. "Well, since I didn't do anything wrong..."

"Didn't do anything—!" She stopped when she saw his smile, and grinned a little. "You're teasing me."

"Well, you're dressed so impeccably, I can't make fun of your clothes." He pulled her closer and said quietly, "I missed you, Steph. I regretted asking you to leave more times...and regretted you actually *going* more times..."

She thawed a little. "I missed you, too. Even though you were a complete jerk."

He gently brushed his lips across hers and felt her shiver. Without warning, her mouth opened beneath his lips and her tongue rubbed against his. He murmured against her mouth and dropped his travel bag to pull her more tightly against him. "Oh, I missed you," he murmured, trying not to clutch at her. God, she felt so good against him, so soft and warm... "I really, really missed you."

"Me, too," she said breathlessly, gasping as he pressed his mouth against her neck. "Even though I was mad at you the whole time, I missed you like crazy."

Reluctantly, he pulled back, finally remembering that they were necking at Gate 42 of the Minneapolis/St. Paul International Airport. His hands were shaking, so he picked up his travel bag to hide the fact.

"Is it just me, or is it super warm in here?" Stephanie asked, trying to catch her breath. She looked flushed and happy.

He grabbed her again and kissed her, hard and quick. "Tomorrow night," he said huskily, looking into her emerald eyes, which were wide and guileless. "Then we'll..."

"Separate the men from the boys," Stephanie giggled, pretending she wasn't thrilling to his touch, to his voice.

"I'll have my way with you and love you until you're silly," he said, sneaking a glance at her. She was still smiling and he reached down to capture her hand. "But I insist you take a shower first. Or maybe I'll bathe you myself."

"Erik..." She could feel her face getting warm. She must have been as red as an apple, because he started laughing at her.

"How were the brook trout biting this morning?" he asked, steering them toward the baggage section.

"Really good! Full creel. We're having them for supper tonight."

"You went fishing without me." He scowled jealously. "Why didn't you wait for me to get here?"

"It was a safety measure," she teased, tracing his scar with a fingertip. He growled a curse and squeezed her until she gasped.

"Maybe we'll ditch the wedding tomorrow and hit Hay Creek instead," he said. "But not the stretch by the cow pasture. I'm an old man, I'm not up to the sprint."

"Chicken," she jeered.

"How am I going to give you babies if I'm lying trampled in the pasture?"

She colored again but rallied gamely. "A good point. We could always use donor—hmm. That's not so funny, I guess."

"Speaking of donors, Brian was asking about you. He and Mother are coming out tonight. I guess Sir has some fancy dinner planned...?"

Stephanie nodded glumly. "Uh-huh. And it's in our honor. I don't think we can get out of it."

"A woman after my own heart."

Back at the house, Sir had prepared the staff and his home as best he could for Stephanie and Erik's arrival. He expected them to storm into the house screaming at the top of their lungs, calling each other vile names, and breaking things. When he heard the car pull into the drive at the front of the house, he hurried down to meet them in the entry hall.

"Get that vase upstairs, quickly," he ordered a passing maid, who complied with speed. He began fumbling for his pipe as the door opened.

"...surprise. No, I won't tell you. No!" Erik laughed, shoving Stephanie, who had been going through his jacket pockets, away. "You'll find out for yourself tomorrow. Hands off in the meantime."

"Oh, come on! Please tell me," she begged. "Is it bigger than a breadbox? Is it bigger than a Mercedes? Hi, Pop."

Sir winced. Stephanie had been experimenting all week.

"Hi, Sir," Erik said easily, jumping as Stephanie dug her hands into his back pocket. "Hey! Will you get lost?"

"He won't tell me what my wedding present is," Stephanie complained, pinching Erik's behind as she dug in his pockets. He twisted around and grabbed her wrists. "Make him tell me, Daddy-o."

The chauffeur came in behind them with Erik's bags and her eyes lit up. "Ah-ha! Hold it, Jimmy," she said, pulling free of Erik. "I need those bags."

Erik grabbed her around the waist as she started toward the

chauffeur, who was grinning and backing away. "Upstairs with those and be sure to lock my door when you come out," he ordered. "Now, you, c'mere." He swung her around and hauled her up against his side. She gasped for breath and poked him in the ribs.

Sir was nonplused. They were acting like any couple in love. They did not seem at all anxious or angry with one another. Just the same, he resolved to keep some of the nicer breakables hidden away, at least until the weekend was over.

"Children," he said. Erik had begun poking Stephanie back and was enjoying himself immensely. "I suggest you get changed and dressed, post haste. Our dinner guests will be arriving in the next couple hours."

Stephanie stuck her tongue out at her father. He raised his eyebrows at her.

Sir sighed. Inside, he was rejoicing. They did love each other, they were just too stubborn to admit it. He remembered overhearing Erik declare his love the night before Stephanie left for Boston. At the time, he had wondered if perhaps the young man's hormones had been doing the talking. Now he knew that was only part of it. "If you two don't behave..."

"We can't come to dinner?" Stephanie asked hopefully.

"I'll make you stay until the very last guest has gone home. And then I'll make you clean up."

They took the stairs two at a time.

Chapter 27

"...HONEYMOON?"

A short silence fell. Stephanie realized with a start that Marceline Chambers had asked her a question.

"I'm sorry?" she asked politely.

Erik kicked her under the table. "Can't you at least pretend to pay attention?" he whispered, grinning.

"I asked where you two are going on your honeymoon," Marceline said again, a little more loudly.

"Honeymoon? Um, we haven't planned that far in advance."

There was another silence. Brian cleared his throat. "Wedding's tomorrow, sweet cakes. When were you figuring on planning for it?"

"We're spending it at Winnawachee Lodge, up by Lake Superior," Erik said.

"Salmon fishing," Sir guessed.

"We are? That sounds great!" Stephanie loved Lake Superior, and this time of the year it would be beautiful up north. "My future husband is a genius."

Erik looked modest. Brian looked amused. Sir sighed and poured himself another glass of wine.

"We'll leave Sunday—or maybe Monday. And stay about two weeks?" she said, looking at Erik. He shrugged. "Yeah. Two weeks. And we'll bring back lots of yummy salmon."

Marceline wrinkled her nose at Stephanie. How such a beautiful, well-bred young lady could get such joy out of...fishing, she didn't know. And she supposed it didn't matter. Her Erik had landed an heiress, that was what counted. Her place in social circles back East was assured. After all, her daughter-in-law was Sir Chesterson's only child. After Brian's birthday party two weeks ago, her social calendar had been completely booked for the next eight months.

She smiled and had another sip of Sir's very excellent wine. Beside her, Brian drank beer.

Stephanie was bored silly. Not only was the conversation stilted for the most part, but she very much disliked her future mother-in-law, and was still feeling a little awkward around Brian. She kept expecting him to turn cold and nasty in response to something she did that might remind him of Veronica.

She sighed and poked at her brook trout. Across the table, Erik noticed his fiancee's disconsolate expression and his heart went out to her. He decided to take the bull by the horns.

"So how did you and Veronica meet, anyway?"

Stephanie held her breath and stared, wide-eyed, at her mother's husband. He looked back, candidly enough, and took a big gulp of his beer.

"Went over to Sir's apartment to borrow some notes. I'd blown off class that day to go to Fenway."

"You like baseball?" Stephanie asked. It was hard to picture this dour man cheering for the Red Sox.

"Sure. Always have." Brian grinned at her and stretched out his long legs. He took another swallow of beer. "My dad used to take me to Fenway practically every weekend, in the summertime. Anyway, I'd skipped class that day—some elementary Economics course, boring as hell—and came sniffing around Sir's place to scarf his notes."

"Luckily for you, I had attended class that morning."

"Right. So I get to his place and knock on the door and who opens the door but this knockout blonde. Wow, what a looker! Like Steph, but not as tall, and with blue eyes instead of green. And glasses, big cat's-eye glasses. And she says to me, 'You must be the plebian'. And I go, 'What?' And she says, 'It's no good, I can't talk him into it, either.' And then she brushes by me and walks out."

"We had just at that moment broken up," Sir said.

"And a good thing, too, 'cause I was gonna get her, one way or the other."

"She was very industrious. And I was not. I was forever trying to persuade her to leave off books for a while and come play."

"You? Wanted to play?" Erik's eyebrows climbed toward his hairline.

"I was young," Sir said dryly.

"Yeah. So I'm so busy asking Sir about the dame that I forgot to get the notes. So the next day—bam! A brainstorm."

"You went to her dorm to get her notes."

"Right. I knew she had taken the class last semester, so I figured, with a little luck and the old Dares charm, I'd snag the notes for the rest of the term as well as a date for Saturday night."

"But she threw you out on your ear."

Brian scowled at Stephanie. "Hey! Who's tellin' this story, anyway? How'd you know?"

"If some smarty boy came sniffing around me trying to get all my notes, I'd toss him out, too," Stephanie said haughtily.

"Oh, yeah? Well, for your information, bright eyes, she did throw me out, but I kept going back. And finally she said that if I didn't miss any more of that piss-poor, boring econ class, she'd go out with me."

"And?"

He sighed. "The things I did for love, man. God! I thought that semester would never end."

"She turned him into one of the top students at the school," Sir said, chuckling. "He ranked tenth in a class of four hundred."

"And Ronnie was second. Man, was she pissed! She was counting on valedictorian. She never listened to me—I always told her, life isn't spelled G.PA."

"And where did you rank, Sir?" Stephanie teased.

"Never mind."

"Way down there," Brian told her. She giggled.

Brian had another beer, stole another glance at Stephanie, and told another story. And another. Finally, in the wee hours of the morning, the five decided to retire. Stephanie was struggling to keep her eyes open, and Marcy, bored, had long ago fallen asleep against Brian's shoulder. He had absently put his arm around her while he talked, a gesture that was not lost on anyone.

"What time's the ceremony?" Brian asked, easing himself out of his chair and shaking his wife awake. "C'mon, kid, we gotta hit the sheets. Wake up, Marce."

"Marcellne," she mumbled, opening her eyes.

"Four o'clock," Stephanie replied, mouth stretching open in a tendon-creaking yawn. "And thank goodness, because I want to sleep in."

"Ceremony and reception right here?"

"Yup. I grew up here, and I always knew I'd be married right on the grounds. Well. Inside, unfortunately. It's a little too chilly for an outdoor wedding."

"Convenient, anyway. Hey, Erik, you can give Stephanie that stuff we were talking about. I'm going to bed."

"What stuff?" Stephanie asked.

"You give it to her," Erik said easily. "You've still got it."

"Oh." Brian looked uncomfortable as he fumbled in his trouser pocket. He brought out a small black box. "Well—Erik said you guys hadn't had any luck findin' rings, so if you wanted, you can have this." He tossed the box to Stephanie, who neatly plucked it out of the air and opened it. Her face went very still when she looked inside. "You don't have to use 'em if you don't want," Brian said hastily. "Makes no difference to me. You probably want to buy your own."

"This—this is for me? For us?" Stephanie looked at him, unbelievingly.

"Well. Yeah. If you want. I don't care."

Sir looked over her shoulder and his eyes widened. "Your wedding bands. And Veronica's engagement ring. I thought—"

"You thought I pitched them when I pitched everything else," Brian said with a humorless smile. "Yeah, well. I didn't. Couldn't. I don't know why...but I don't need them anymore. And Ronnie sure don't. So you guys can have them."

"They're beautiful," Stephanie said, speaking with great difficulty. She did not want to embarrass Brian, so she swallowed her tears. Erik was mercifully silent beside her. "I can't tell you how much it means to me to have something of my mother's. It was kind of you to think of us."

"Been collecting dust in my wall safe for twenty years. It was either give them to you or pitch them."

"You're a liar," Stephanie said, making it sound like an endearment. "Thank you, Brian. It's the nicest gift I've ever received." She laughed a little. "The stone is a blue topaz."

"Yeah. It was the only set I could afford," Brian said with a self-deprecating shrug. "Ronnie liked it well enough."

She slipped the ring on her finger. The fit was near-perfect. Plain gold band, blue topaz center stone, two small diamonds on each side of the stone. Nothing fancy, but certainly pleasing to the eye. The wedding bands were plain gold circles. "Thank you again, Brian. Good night." She turned and fled up the stairs. Erik said good night and went after her, leaving Sir, Marceline, and Brian looking after them.

"Kids," Brian said with a shrug, and took his wife to bed.

Erik reached Stephanie's bedroom and had barely taken two steps past the threshold when she hurled herself into his arms.

She sobbed against Erik's chest, getting him quite wet, but he didn't mind. He soothed her as best he could while she wailed that she wasn't crying because she was sad, heavens no, it was that she was so happy she didn't know what to do with herself.

"I know," he said. He waited for her to taper from sobs to hiccups.

"Wasn't that just the nicest, nicest thing he could have done?" she asked, taking the proffered tissue. "Except for my quilt I don't have anything that was Mama's."

"Uh-huh. Here, you missed one." He pulled her close and kissed away the rogue tear. She clung to him and hiccupped, feeling safe.

Much later, she said quietly, "I assume you don't mind if we take his gift?"

"No, of course not."

"It does solve a few problems, doesn't it? I mean, me and you, we just couldn't agree on a..."

"Shush," he said, and kissed her again. "Just shush for a minute, magpie, let me kiss you." His tongue delved into her mouth and she whimpered, clutching at him. He kicked the door shut behind them and got the lights with a blow of his fist against the switch. The room plunged into darkness. "Just let me....let me kiss you, God, Steph, you drive me crazy, let me just..."

She brought him to the carpet with a deft leg sweep, letting herself fall with him, gasping in surprise as he rolled over so she was lying full-length on top of him. He pulled her head down and kissed her, while the other hand was busy at her blouse. She sucked in breath as his hand slipped inside her bra, lightly kneading the tender flesh, thumb stroking across the nipple.

She shrugged the blouse off and was reaching around to unsnap her bra when he hauled her to her feet and tossed her in the general direction of the bed. His breathing sounded very loud in the dark.

She stumbled against the bed and he was right behind her, steadying her as he unsnapped her bra and reached around to cup her breasts. She groaned and her knees tried to buckle, but he held her up against him, lips against her ear, her throat.

"You are all the beauty in this world," he said, and she thought she might weep.

"You can't see me," she managed. She arched against him as he caressed her breasts, her stomach.

"I can feel you." He inched her skirt up and groaned aloud when he felt the garter belt and stockings. "Damned Victoria's Secret junk," he growled. "I forbid you to buy anything there ever again. It's too hard to keep my hands off you when you prance around in this stuff."

"I know," she giggled.

"Oh, you do, do you?" His hand, moving between her thighs, stroking across the lace that shielded her curly mound from him. He bent her over until her hands were braced against the bed.

"What are you...doing?" His hands. His hands, running up and down her inner thighs, reaching around to stroke her stiffened nipples, giveaways to how his touch was affecting her, his lips kissing her shoulders, the back of her neck. Her legs weren't going to support her much longer.

"You like getting me hot? Running around in little lace nothings? Preying on my self control?" His laughter swirled around her in the dark room. Deep laughter, almost chuckling as he stroked and caressed and kissed. "Well, my demure virginal wife-to-be, let's see how you like it."

He unsnapped the garter belt, but left the stockings. "Kick off your shoes," he growled, and she obeyed. Part of her was a little worried, wondering if she was in over her head—*knowing* she was in over her head—but she instinctively knew he would never harm her. She waited.

His fingers slipped past the elastic band, felt her damp heat. Stephanie shuddered.

"Oh, yes," he murmured. His fingers stroked, the other hand reached up and cupped a breast. His darling, his lovely, hot, achingly sensuous darling was trembling and moaning and he loved her so much he thought he might die from the wonder of it.

He was wild to have her, but oddly enough, it was sufficient to pleasure her for now. In a different way, it was as satisfying as his own pleasure. Touching her was another kind of ecstasy.

He slipped a finger into her tight, hot sheath. She bucked against him; he held her bent over, braced against the bed, and stroked her with thorough, agonizing slowness.

"No," she whimpered. "Oh, God. Please don't. Do this to me."

He slipped his finger out and rubbed it across the sensitive nub of her clitoris. "You're so hot and wet," he murmured.

"Er-r-r-r-rik," she groaned, fisting the bedspread. She felt his finger slide into her again and wanted to scream with frustration. He was driving her mad. "Oh, God, please, I—"

He was inching her panties down with agonizing slowness, murmuring soothing nothings to her. She didn't want to be soothed. She wanted to be his, thoroughly his, and she wanted it now, dammit.

His hands were caressing her bare buttocks, sliding under to cup her in his hands. His hands slid further until a finger was slipping inside her again.

"You're so tight," he said with something like wonder in his voice. "It will be difficult for me to hold back, tomorrow night. Just feeling you around me will send me over the edge, I'm quite sure. Why, love, you're shaking like a leaf. Are you cold?"

"You bastard," she said raggedly.

"Tsk, tsk," he murmured. His finger began sliding in and out. Her knees buckled and this time he let her go; she fell forward onto the bed. She felt his hand on the small of her back, holding her in place, felt his fingers busy between her thighs, heard him speaking to her quietly.

She sobbed, nearly clawing at the bedspread, so overwhelmed by desire she thought she might die. If she didn't find release soon, she hoped she would die.

His hands, his wonderful, glorious, skilled hands, pulled away and she sobbed again. She felt his hands on her shoulders, rolling her onto her back.

"Please," she said weakly, breathing so hard she was almost panting. He was looking at her, and there was great tenderness in his eyes. "Please. Please." She clutched at his shirt. "Erik, I want you so much, but I don't know what—"

"Tell me you love me," he murmured, freeing himself from her grasp.

"Erik—"

"Tell me you love me and I'll help you."

"I can't," she said, beginning to cry.

"Please!" he shouted, hands on her shoulders, nearly shaking her in his need. "Please, Steph, I need to hear it. It's okay if you don't—"

"I can't!" she cried, and the raw agony in her voice halted his own pleas. "I can't or you'll think I'm only saying it in the heat of the moment. You won't know I mean it."

He was still as stone for a moment, then whispered, "Just say it, sweetheart, and we'll worry about the rest in the morning."

"I love you, Erik." She paused and touched his cheek. "I've loved you forever—oh!"

His hands were busy again, but this time he was sliding down her stomach and in seconds his mouth was pleasuring her as well as his fingers. She cried out, sobbing his name and tugging on fistfuls of his hair, then reached blindly for him as she came back to earth from her climax. He quickly disrobed to his shorts and pulled her into his arms. "Help me," he said shakily. "Help me if you still want to be a virgin tomorrow."

"Yes. Yes," she gasped. "Tell me what you like—can I touch you?"

He gasped an affirmative and nearly found release the moment her hand slipped down the waistband of his shorts.

"I don't know what to do. I don't want to hurt you. God, you feel like—like silk," she said softly, wonderingly. "Like velvet, like steel velvet."

Her eyes had adjusted to the dark, she could see his head was thrown back, the cords on his neck standing out, teeth gritted. Instinct guided her fingers and she stroked his lovely long length. This part of him was hot and pulsed against her hand. She was blackly excited at feel of him, at the effect her touch had on him. "Is that good? Should I do something else?"

"I love you, too," he gasped out, crushing his mouth down on hers. She wriggled and kissed him back, stroking his length and marveling at how very different he was from she. She wasn't afraid, but she did wonder—he was so big, how would they fit tomorrow night? "Oh, God, I'm close," he moaned against her mouth. "Please don't stop. Please. Don't. St—Stop. Stephanie. Stephanie. Love you. Please."

Her other hand slid down and gently cupped his testicles, and that simple motion brought him release. He shook with the force of his orgasm and she held him until it was over.

"Stephanie," he said at last, and to his total surprise his cheeks were wet.

"Shush," she said, licking his tears away and kissing him. "We'll worry about it in the morning. Bleah, you made a mess. Go to sleep, if you can."

He did, almost immediately, and she lay in the dark, her own tears running down her cheeks unchecked.

We did it, she thought dazedly. We said the words.

She knew that saying them during lovemaking was one thing. Saying it when they were both vertical would be quite another.

"Tomorrow's project," she murmured, and went to sleep, cuddling Erik against her like the world's biggest doll.

Chapter 28

STEPHANIE opened her eyes to see a disapproving Sir standing over her. With a surge of embarrassment, she realized Erik was still beside her, insensible, and both of them were in a state of dishabille.

"It's not what you're thinking," she told Sir, stifling a yawn, feeling her cheeks grow warm. She checked to make sure they were both decently covered.

"It most certainly is. You're both late, is what I am thinking, and I am right. It is nearly noon."

"What, is the bride still in bed?" Brian asked, coming into the room. He stopped short when he saw his stepson deeply asleep beside Stephanie.

"I should have locked my door," she mumbled, scarlet.

"You sure should have. Just look what happens when you don't. Midnight guests." Brian prodded his stepson with the toe of his Oxford. "Get up, you lazy slug. Time to get married and make an honest woman out of my almost-daughter."

"I am an honest woman," Stephanie said. "Let him sleep. Bed-sharing doth not a deflowering make."

Brian hooted laughter. "What, like you're still a virgin? Good God, you're twenty-three years old! Practically an old maid."

"I'm relieved to hear it," Sir said.

"You're an old-fashioned moron," Brian replied, amiably enough.

"Will you all get out of here?" Stephanie screeched. Erik opened his eyes at the sound and started when he saw Brian and Sir leaning over them.

"What the hell?" he asked muzzily. "Steph, cover up."

"I am."

"Good. You two—out. We'll be along directly."

"You're coming with us, boy-o. Bad luck to see the bride before the wedding."

"I already have," Erik pointed out, stretching. He grabbed Stephanie by the nape of the neck and kissed her, then got up.

"Nice shorts," Brian said.

"Thank you," Erik replied with dignity, as if he were being complimented on the cut of his tuxedo rather than the state of his underwear. "See you later, hon."

"G'bye," Stephanie said, yawning again. Brian escorted Erik out and Sir sat on the edge of her bed.

"Uh—Sir, I'd really like to get up and get dressed."

"Plenty of time for that. How are you feeling?"

"Fine," Stephanie said, mystified. "Of course, I just got up."

"Indeed. The caterers got here an hour ago, the florist was here after breakfast, and everything has been set up downstairs."

"Great."

"But I can send them all away, if that is your wish."

"What? Don't be silly. I mean, that's not my wish."

He looked her over carefully, his gaze finally resting on a pair of wide green eyes, completely guileless and more than a little puzzled.

"It is no trouble, calling off a wedding," he said. "I just pay them as I would have and it goes away."

"I love him," Stephanie said simply.

"Really? I mean...yes, of course you do."

"All my complaints and worries and all the rest...it's just talk. I love him and I know he loves me. Yesterday...well, we got a lot of things cleared up. We're pretty much stuck with each other." She smiled, a big sunny smile that showed she wasn't terribly perturbed at such a fate.

"I am very glad to hear it. I think your mother would be very proud, seeing you today. Seeing you and Erik."

"And Brian, the jerk," Stephanie said, smiling.

"He is as abrasive as always. It is what your mother liked about him. I can't imagine why."

"No wonder you two broke up."

"Indeed." He leaned forward and kissed Stephanie's brow. "I am very proud of you. And I love you very much."

"I know." She swallowed the lump in her throat and willed herself not to cry. "I know you do, Father."

He pulled back and seemed to mull that over. "Father. Simple. Direct. Understated. Yes, I like it."

"Good. I love you, too. Did I tell you you're giving me away?"

"Yes."

"Good. And now I really should get dressed."

"Of course. May I ask you a very blunt question?"

Sir? Blunt? Not in this lifetime. "Yeah, sure."

"Are you really still a virgin?"

"Sir!"

"Sorry," he said hastily, getting up. "It is just...in this day in age—I am pleased, but surprised. Did you get too much sun yesterday? You seem a little flushed."

"Out!"

"As you wish," he said and beat a hasty retreat. So hasty, that Stephanie didn't hear him chuckling on the way out.

Much later, Sir came upstairs to fetch the bride. He was flawlessly attired in one of his tuxedos, but ruined the effect by repeatedly going through his pockets, looking for his tobacco pouch. He knew it wasn't there but long habit would not be denied.

"Are you ready, bride?" he asked, tapping the closed door.

"Is everything ready to go?" Stephanie asked.

"Yes indeed. We await your appearance, that is all."

She flung the door open, clutching her bouquet. "Great. Let's get this show on the road. Do I look okay?" She paused, gauging his reaction. "Well? Do I? Father? Sir? Hello?"

Sir stared at the vision before him. Stephanie had been concerned that the sight of her in a traditional wedding gown might upset Brian and Sir, so great a resemblance did she bear to Veronica. With that in mind, she had selected a knee-length, white silk dress with short sleeves. The dress was in two layers, silk underneath, and white lace in a rose pattern on top. Stephanie had caught her hair back from her face with a wide white ribbon, letting the golden waves spill down her back. White sheer stockings and low-heeled pumps completed the picture.

"Well, I was never one for yards and yards of dress, you know," she said, amused at Sir's—unflappable Sir!—reaction. "I'm nervous as hell. Do I look it?"

"You look extraordinary," Sir said in a barely audible voice.

"Thanks." She smiled. "I hope Erik thinks so. Ready to go?"

"Yes."

"Here we go, then," Stephanie said. She took his arm and a deep breath. So excited and nervous was she that she forgot she was holding her breath until her head began to pound. She expelled her lungs with a gasp. "I'm fine," she muttered before her father—how nice that sounded!—could ask.

She had chosen the main hall for the ceremony. It was a large, airy room, uncluttered with expensive gew-gaws. Its finest attributes were a ceiling-high mirror on one end and a mahogany staircase on the other. The staircase was six feet wide and two floors high. They would be coming into the room from the second floor.

Dear God, Stephanie prayed, please don't let me trip.

On the first level, waiting for Stephanie, Erik casually surveyed the guests. There were about thirty, some friends of Sir's, Brian and Marceline, the household staff, and Annabell Lousilito, who, according to Marceline, wouldn't have let wild horses keep her away. Annabell, it seemed, had taken a great interest in Sir's daughter.

He was impressed with the decorating job. When Stephanie left him in anger and sadness two weeks ago, he had assumed she wouldn't have the time or the inclination to make many arrangements in the short time allotted them. But she had and quite a job it was, too.

The hall was festooned with red tulips and white roses. Everything was spotless and carefully arranged. The dining room, which Erik had peeked in at earlier, looked indescribably elegant, with fine linens and crystals on every table, masses of tulips and roses as table centerpieces, and the entire room lit by candle light. He could hardly believe that such understated decorations could be so beautiful. Such a refreshing change from clutter—even expensive clutter.

It warmed him, the effort she had made. It told him she cared. No matter what the outside pretenses to their marriage were, she wanted her wedding day to be beautiful, and so it would be.

And maybe the pretenses were fast losing their place in this arrangement. Last night...surely she had meant what she had said?

The gardener, doing double duty as a pianist, struck up with the chords of "Here Comes the Bride". Erik looked to the head of the staircase, and his mouth dropped open.

Beside him, Brian gasped.

Stephanie descended, holding Sir's arm, with the grace of a queen. She spotted the two of them standing by the judge and ruined the effect by waving vigorously.

"Holy God," Brian muttered. He clutched Erik's arm in a grip of iron. "You lucked out, boy. Don't screw it up."

"I won't," Erik managed. He couldn't take his eyes off his bride. She was so beautiful, it nearly hurt to look at her. And more than beautiful. She was kind, and loving and generous, and she had a sense of humor, and she wouldn't let him be an ass. She was...hell, she was perfect.

"Who gives this woman?" the judge murmured, smiling.

"I do," Sir replied and handed her off to Erik.

"I feel like a baton," Stephanie muttered as she took Erik's outstretched hand.

"You sure don't look like one," Brian offered. Stephanie flashed him one of her 5000 volt smiles and the man puffed up.

They began. It would be a short ceremony. They had written their own vows, and, facing each other, Erik began.

"You're the greatest thing I ever stumbled across," he said in a firm, clear voice that carried across the hall with no trouble. Beside him, Brian snickered. "I don't know why you'd want a jerk like me, but you do, and I'm forever grateful. I'll try hard to be worthy of you. I promise not to cheat on you. I'll never try to keep you further than a five hour plane trip from your father. I'll never try to buy your favors. I'll try not to grouch at you when I'm upset about something. I'll try not to be jealous of your fly casting." A few titters from the audience. Here came the sticky part. He took a deep breath and said, "I have loved you from the moment I first saw you, I love you now, and I'll always love you. I swear it."

Stephanie stared at him.

Everyone waited.

Stephanie stared at him.

The judge cleared her throat. "Stephanie Veronica...?"

Still she stared. She looked at her hands for a moment, then looked up. Erik was shocked to see a single tear tracking down her cheek.

"I promise to be as good a wife as I can," she began in a low voice.

He tightened his grip on her hands and said, "You don't have to fin—"

She shook her head. Tears flew. "I promise to be as good a wife as I can," she repeated, louder. "I promise to be a good mother to your children. I'll never stray and I'll try hard to be patient when you're grouching at me because you're in a bad mood. And—I love you, too." The bride burst into tears and stomped on the groom's foot. "You ruined it!" she sobbed, while Erik grimaced and clutched at his shoe. "I was going to say I love you first, so you wouldn't be afraid."

Gingerly touching his foot to the floor, he said to the judge, "Finish it."

"I now pronounce you man and wife," the judge said, mystified.

"Hear that, Steph? We're married. You can't undo it, so you might as well make the best of it."

"I meant to say it a long time ago," Stephanie said, kissing her husband, still crying. "But I was afraid—"

"You were afraid I'd be a real jerk," he said, kissing her back. "Rightly so. I love you, Steph."

"You better!" she cried. "After all the crap we've put each other through, you just better!"

"Well then," Sir said quietly.

"Can we eat?" Brian asked, uncomfortable with all the tear-shedding and love words. "Want me to get you an ice pack, Erik?"

Erik declined and they did not immediately eat. First, the bride and groom had to be petted and kissed by the guests. Annabell in particular fussed over them and promised to feed all the wedding details to one of Boston's gossip columnists. Marceline was polite and had been for the last forty-eight hours, so Stephanie was content with that. Brian was in good humor and extravagantly complimentary.

"You look great, kiddo. Your ma was a beautiful woman, but I think you mighta beat the band by a little bit. And what a dress! You look good enough to run around the track."

"Thank you," Stephanie replied, wondering if that was good or bad.

"So this is the little woman?" an unfamiliar voice said. The bride and groom turned.

Erik visibly jumped. "Margaret!"

"Your old girlfriend?" Stephanie asked, eating the woman up with her eyes.

"Ah, he's told you about me." Margaret was a small redhead, holding hands with her date, a tall, blue-eyed brunette. "My wife, Maureen."

"Your...wife?" Erik sounded as if he were choking. Stephanie was openly grinning. Behind them, Marceline looked smug.

"I'm...pleased to meet you, Mrs.—err, Maurine. My wife, Stephanie."

"Oooh, I like the way that sounds," Stephanie said.

"I would have hated the way it sounds," Margaret said. "I suppose it's why things didn't work out between us."

"One of the reasons," Marceline said dryly.

"You—" Erik still sounded as if he were choking. Stephanie elbowed him in the ribs and treated Margaret and Maureen to a large smile.

"So glad you could make it. Dinner will be in a few minutes. I hope you can stay the night."

"Oh, we will. We will." She grinned. "Nice seeing you again, Chambers." She walked away, Maureen in tow. Erik whirled on his mother.

"You knew, didn't you?"

Marceline shrugged and tried to look less smug, with no luck.

"You wouldn't have believed me if I told you she was only with you for the money. So I proved it. She took the money and ran. I told her about the wedding. I assumed curiosity would compel her to make an appearance."

"I don't know whether to kiss you or strangle you."

"Kiss me instead and be nice to your mother," Stephanie instructed. "Marceline, you're a terribly bad girl."

"No, just a terribly practical one." She jumped as Brian goosed her from behind. "Brian! Behave yourself. We're at your son's wedding."

"He's no son of mine," Brian grumped and goosed his wife again. "Good thing, too. I can take advantage of him in business and not feel too bad."

"Ha," Erik said sourly.

They chatted with the other guests and snacked on shrimp cocktail. "Do you like the flowers?" Stephanie asked, surveying the room with satisfaction. "Tulips are my favorite."

"You did a terrific job."

"Thanks, but I had lots of help. You're right, though, the place looks beautiful. Where are we going?"

Erik was steering her up the stairs. "We have some business to tend to," he said casually, and she let herself be propelled.

In the center of her bed was a medium-sized, square box, gaily wrapped. In seconds, she had the paper off and was exclaiming over her gift. "A tackle box! Wow! My old one's all beat up. Thanks, Erik!"

"Open it," he said, smiling over her pleasure. Behind him, he thumbed the lock to her door.

"Fishing lures! Oooh, all the good ones, too. Hey, and you've got the red and white ones! They're the best." She lifted up the tray and spotted the envelope. She opened it and burst out laughing. "My very own bait and tackle shop! Oh, Erik...I don't know what to say. What a perfect present!" She bounded from the bed and grabbed the envelope on her dresser, handing it to him with a flourish. "Here's yours."

He opened it and read the deed. Puzzled, he said, "It says I'm the proud owner of some land, but what—" He read it again and began to laugh. "Hay Creek!"

"Not all of it," Stephanie said quickly. "Just the stretch by the cow pasture. I finally bought out the farmer. He was happy enough to sell, especially for the money I was offering. I thought we could get some exercise."

"Shameless wench," he said, snatching at her. She shrieked

laughter and tried to pull back. "I love you, sweetheart."

"I love you, too. I'm so happy, Erik, I can't even put into words how I feel."

"You don't have to," he replied somberly, looking into her incredible eyes. "I feel the same way. You've set me free, Stephanie. I was well on the way to becoming a sour old man, but you saved me from that."

"You didn't need saving. You just needed a nudge. Someone would have shown you. I'm just glad I got to you first."

She kissed him, tentatively at first, then whimpering a little as his tongue plundered her mouth. His hands roamed her silk-clad body and she felt as if her heart rate had just doubled.

"Oh, Stephanie. I've waited so long. I've wanted and loved you forever."

"No, I've wanted *you*, and loved you forever."

He found her zipper and pulled. The fabric parted at her back and the gown puddled at her feet. He held her arms out and looked at her for a long time.

"You're perfect," he said at last. "Will it take you very long to quit blushing? Because I'm not turning the light off this time. I want to see you."

She stared at him, then bent to pick up her dress. "Now? Don't be silly. We've got a roomful of guests downstairs, and we'll be having dinner soon, they're probably waiting for us..."

"We're married now," he said firmly, pushing her into a sitting position on the bed and bending down to take off her shoes. "I'm not waiting another second."

"For God's sake, the ink on our marriage certificate is barely dry!" she protested, trying to pretend she didn't want him, trying to pretend his touch wasn't affecting her. She groaned as he pulled off her stockings. "Are you listening to me?"

"No," he smiled, shrugging out of his jacket. In moments, he was undressed. He didn't stop at his shorts this time.

She looked at him for a long while, satisfying her curiosity. She had never seen him unclothed. He was all muscle and tanned skin. "You're beautiful," she said at last. She met his gaze. "So strong and...hard. All over, you're hard. I'm all soft and mushy, bleah."

"You're soft, yes, but it's hardly bleah." Suddenly he was there, pulling her into his arms and she clung to him as they kissed. He pulled her toward him until she was lying on top, then undid the hook and eyes of her bustier. "Very nice," he breathed as her breasts swung free.

He caught a stiffening nipple between his teeth, smiling at Stephanie's gasp. "I love the way you respond to me."

"I can't help it," she groaned as he rolled her over on her back.

"I don't want you to help it, nitwit. Here, let me...how's that?"

His hands. Did she love him for his sterling personality or his wonderfully skilled hands? Right now, she couldn't decide. "I love your hands on me," she groaned. "Let me touch you." She ran her hands over his chest, then leaned up to kiss a nipple. His sharply indrawn breath pleased her. She reached down to clasp him and he nearly fell off the bed.

"I can't get over how you feel!" Stephanie exclaimed. "So hard and—and smooth."

"Aaaggh!" He grabbed her hand. "Stop that or we'll be finished before we've started." He slid his hands beneath her, lifted her up, then inched her panties off. He ran his fingers through the soft curls between her legs, curls moist with her desire. "You feel so pretty," he murmured, capturing her mouth for another searing kiss. She arched up against his hand as he stroked the slick folds, gently inserting a finger to gauge her readiness. She gasped against his mouth. "Oh, wait—I want to taste you." He trailed kisses down her neck, across her breasts, pausing to suckle one for a few sweet moments, then rained kisses down her stomach. He felt her fingers twine in his hair and fist, then kissed her very center.

"Erik," she moaned. "Oh, God. Please don't stop. I—oh, how I love you!"

"Let me—here." She could feel his hands on her thighs, spreading her legs apart. His mouth, kissing her, kissing her there, his tongue flicking so sweetly quick. "God, you taste marvelous." He eased a finger inside of her, at the same time tonguing the sensitive nub of her clitoris.

"Erik!" she screamed. Heat uncoiled in her belly and raced through her limbs. There was an explosion in her loins and she could feel herself arching against him as her orgasm claimed her. "Erik," she said again, breath coming in harsh gasps as she fell back.

Suddenly he was leaning over her, kissing her with urgent, almost frantic need. She nearly found release again as she tasted herself on his lips. She could feel his manhood probing between her thighs and nearly gasped at the wonder of it. She reached down to clasp him, to help him, and his fingers bit into her arms as he shuddered. "Just...ah, God! Here, let me—"

He slipped into her with excruciating sweetness. She instinctively arched up, accepting more of her, and felt him stop.

"Wait—don't—what's the matter?"

"I don't want to hurt you. Please—it's your first time and I'm enough of a pig to be glad I'm the one, but this might—might—"

He was having trouble thinking clearly. Her eyes were so wide and trusting and, God help him, puzzled. She felt so hot and tight, he was having trouble forming words to prepare her. With a groan of frustration he surged forward and nearly wept when Stephanie cried out.

"Ouch, dammit!" She was squirming beneath him, frightened at the pain and, no doubt, pissed as hell.

"Don't move, don't move!"

"I can't," she said, and now she was crying. He thought his heart would break at the sight of those tears. "You've got me pinned like a butterfly to a board. Erik, it hurts."

"I know," he groaned. She was all around him, clenched so hot and tight, and the urge to slam in and out of her tender body until he found release was nearly overwhelming. "Please stay still. It won't hurt for long."

"All right," she said in a very small voice, reaching up to wipe away her tears. Stupid damn tears. It was her wedding day, Erik was making love to her, so what if it did hurt a little? No reason to act like a big baby. But it had felt so nice and now oh how it hurt...she hadn't known it would hurt.

He kissed her softly, then more urgently. His tongue swept inside to mate with hers and he settled against her, determined to wait—even if it killed him—until she was ready.

Her eyes, which had been closed while he kissed her, opened wide. "Oh, my!" she said. When he had moved a little, settling himself while he kissed her, the pain had lessened dramatically. It was almost as if a switch had been thrown. She was suddenly very conscious of his throbbing length, embedded in her heat, making her feel very...strange. "Oh, my!" she said again, feeling a little silly at how inadequate she sounded. "Erik, I—" Experimentally, she moved against him. The feeling was so amazingly pleasurable, so incredibly intimate, that she almost cried again, this time at the wonder of it.

"That's it, sweet," he breathed. He grasped her hips and pulled her against him. She gasped and her eyes slipped closed. "Oh, yes, that's it, just let yourself go."

He pulled back, and then thrust forward. He pulled back again, then felt her legs lock behind him and force him forward again. She was squirming beneath him, making little cries in her throat that were as exciting to him as her movements. "Oh, Erik, that feels so—so good and so strange, I—"

He kissed her again, stifling her cries, which were getting louder and louder as she approached orgasm. His own was near, the feel of her tight sheath around him enough to put him over the edge.

Suddenly, she bucked against him, arching up and up, crying his name over and over. He found his own release then, pouring his seed into her with a groan of surrender.

He collapsed against her, his harsh breathing mingling with hers, quicker and lighter.

"My God," he said at last.

"Erik, that was amazing," she said. "Is it always like that?"

"It has never been like that. Not for me."

"Oh. Well, me neither, obviously." A pause, then, brightly: "Can we do it again?"

He groaned and rolled away, grabbing the blankets and covering them up. "After dinner," he said, wondering if he would live that long.

"That long?" She smiled at him, he saw she was teasing. "I would like to wait awhile, too. I'm a little sore. But not too long. I love you."

"Me too. I'm glad we waited, though at times I thought I was going to go crazy. I wanted you so badly..."

"I know," she said smugly. "I thought that was the only thing you liked about me. I'm glad that's not so."

"Well..." he said, then dodged as she pretended to slap him, laughing. He kissed her again and pulled her close. Tracing a finger along her fine eyebrows, he murmured, "What I can't figure out is where you got these incredible eyes. Veronica had blue eyes, remember?"

"Mmm hmm." She started as someone knocked on the door.

"Sorry to interrupt, but dinner is ready. Is everything all right?" Sir called.

"Everything's great," Stephanie giggled. "Erik locked the door, Father."

"What a pest," Erik muttered. "Can't deflower my own damn wife without him poking his nose in."

"Indeed. Cover up, I've got a key."

The door opened and Sir peered in at them. "For heaven's sake!" he said, shaking his head. "The ink on your marriage certificate is barely dry."

"That's what I told him," Stephanie began, blushing furiously, but

Erik sat bolt upright, mouth agape. "Erik, what's the matter?"

"Sir!" he said, flabbergasted.

"What?" Sir replied, mystified.

"You've got *green eyes!*"

"So he does," Stephanie said wonderingly. "I never really noticed before."

She caught Erik's glance and they both burst out laughing. Sir shut the door on them, admonishing them to get up and get dressed, but they were so busy kissing each other they didn't hear.

~*~

MaryJanice Davidson

MaryJanice Davidson writes across a variety of genres, including young adult, paranormal, inspirational, non-fiction, and erotica. She won the Sapphire Award in 2001, was a P.E.A.R.L. finalist, and won the All About Romance Reader's Choice award for best novella.

MaryJanice lives in Minnesota with her husband, Anthony, and their two children. She loves getting e-mails from readers at: alongi@usinternet.com

For information on her other award-winning books, check out her website at: www.usinternet.com/users/alongi/index.html

Printed in the United States
25122LVS00001B/120

9 780759 900639